"Look at me," D

 She did so, and foun

"Help me, Sally. Say you agree," he said softly, his breath whispering against her face.

"But—"

"Say it. For my son's sake."

"All right. I agree."

Slowly Damiano dropped his head until his mouth brushed hers. She held herself steady, waiting for it to be over, feeling the tremors go through her, fighting every instinct that urged her to press against him and tempt him on—and on....

His lips parted from hers, but she could still feel the warmth of his breath. She tried to force her mind to take control. Damiano's kiss had a power over her that she must fight. But her flesh challenged her, telling her mind that thoughts were irrelevant. The only thing that mattered was the sweetness flooding through her, destroying the common sense that had always ruled her life.

His eyes told her that he'd felt her tremble in his arms and knew his power over her. Now nothing could ever be the same. He would force on her a kiss of passion that would leave her no choice. She braced herself— part fearful, part furious, part craving.

She ought to leave Venice, she thought. She couldn't bear to hurt the child, but it was better for him not to indulge in groundless hopes. But another voice spoke within her, urging her to marry Damiano and put her whole heart and soul into winning his love.

Dear Reader,

A convenient wedding is rarely a matter of convenience alone. Secretly both bride and groom are hoping for something more. Sally, my heroine, is haunted by many thoughts and dreams as she walks down the aisle in Venice, to marry according to the traditions of the city.

Venice has been a special place to me ever since the day I took a holiday there, met a charming Venetian man and became engaged to him in two days. Many years later we are still happily married. I learned then that I was a different person from the one I'd thought. I'd seen myself as cautious, reserved—the last person to fall in love at first sight and make an impulsive marriage. Yet in that magical city my new self took over.

Sally also discovers in Venice that she has several different selves, which lead her to the love that was always fated for her. Just as mine was fated for me.

Suddenly I—an only child—found myself a member of a large family who opened their arms to me with warmth and generosity. I was particularly drawn to Carla, my husband's sister, who said to me a year ago, "When are you going to set another book in Venice? It's been too long since your last one."

That very evening I was working out the plot and looking forward to showing the book to Carla, who'd inspired it. Sadly, I was never able to do so. As I was finishing the last chapter the news came of her death.

All I can do now is dedicate the book to her, which I'm glad to do. It's hers, and it always will be.

Lucy

Not Just a Convenient Marriage

—

Lucy Gordon

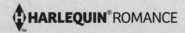
HARLEQUIN®ROMANCE

Recycling programs
for this product may
not exist in your area.

ISBN-13: 978-0-373-74301-8

NOT JUST A CONVENIENT MARRIAGE

First North American Publication 2014

Printed in U.S.A.

HARLEQUIN®
www.Harlequin.com

Lucy Gordon cut her writing teeth on magazine journalism, interviewing many of the world's most interesting men, including Warren Beatty, Charlton Heston and Roger Moore. She also camped out with lions in Africa, and had many other unusual experiences, which have often provided the background for her books. Several years ago, while staying in Venice, she met a Venetian who proposed in two days. They have been married ever since. Naturally this has affected her writing, in which romantic Italian men tend to feature strongly.

Two of her books have won a Romance Writers of America RITA® Award. You can visit her website at www.lucy-gordon.com.

Recent books by Lucy Gordon:

THE FINAL FALCON SAYS I DO*
FALLING FOR THE REBEL FALCON*
PLAIN JANE IN THE SPOTLIGHT*
MISS PRIM AND THE BILLIONAIRE*
RESCUED BY THE BROODING TYCOON*
HIS DIAMOND BRIDE
A MISTLETOE PROPOSAL

*The Falcon Dynasty

This and other titles by Lucy Gordon are available in ebook format from www.Harlequin.com.

I dedicate this book to Carla, my Venetian sister-in-law, who made the light-hearted remark that inspired me to write it.

CHAPTER ONE

'WOW! CASANOVA! FANCY that!'

The young man devouring the contents of a book was alight with excitement. Sally, his sister, sitting beside him in the plane, regarded him curiously.

'What are you on about, Charlie?'

'Casanova, the great lover. He came from Venice. It says so here.' He held up the tourist booklet about the city. 'He had a thousand women and gambled a fortune every night.'

'Then I can see why he attracts you,' she said wryly.

At eighteen, Charlie had gambling debts that were fast mounting, something that barely troubled him while he could rely on his sister to stump up. But Sally had rebelled. Appalled by his developing addiction and the fearsome characters who were beginning to haunt their home, she'd hurriedly got him out of London. Now they were on a plane approaching Venice in what looked like a holiday but was actually an escape.

'It's not just the gambling,' Charlie said. 'He could have any woman he wanted, and they say that even now his legend lives in Venice. Aw, come on, that should interest you.'

'Shut it!' Sally told him.

His manner became comically theatrical. 'How can you be so hard-hearted? You're going to the most romantic city in the world and you couldn't care less.'

'Just as you couldn't care less about the trouble your gambling causes. You're only trying to change the subject. So just drop it, little brother. Or else!'

'Or else what? Throw me out of the plane?'

'No, I'll do something much worse than that. I'll cut off the money and make you get a job.'

'Aaargh! You're a cruel woman.'

Their tone was light, but beneath the banter was a hard reality. Since their parents had died seven years earlier she'd been responsible for him. She wasn't proud of the result. He showed no signs of growing up.

As he'd said, they were travelling to the most romantic city in the world: Venice. Over a hundred little islands, connected by canals and bridges. A place of staggering beauty and magical, romantic atmosphere. And if she 'couldn't care less' as he accused, it might be because there had been little romance in her life. Without being exactly plain she had looks that were ordinary, with nothing enchanting or alluring about them. Men did not tend to fall at her feet, and the one time she'd fancied herself in love there had been little happiness, and pain in the end. She had no illusions that her life was about to change now.

'Why did you insist on coming to Venice when we could have gone anywhere?' Charlie persisted.

'Because I had a friend who'd booked a trip here and had to cancel at the last minute,' she said. 'I managed to get her hotel rooms, and air tickets.'

She had seized the offer as a chance to get away fast and cheaply. Otherwise she wouldn't have chosen to make this trip in January.

A voice on the loudspeaker announced that the descent was about to start. Soon they could see Marco Polo Airport near the boundary of the mainland. Close by was the sea, with the two-mile causeway stretching out over the water to the multitude of little islands that made up the city of Venice.

'Hang on,' said Charlie. 'It says here that there are no cars in Venice. Does that mean we have to walk along that causeway?'

'No, there's a car park called Piazzale Roma on the very edge of the city,' she said. 'A taxi can take us as far as that, then we get out and do the rest of the journey by boat through the canals.'

As they descended she gazed out of the window, enchanted by the glittering sea stretching out to where Venice could just be glimpsed on the horizon. When they landed there was the relief of finding a plentiful supply of taxis, and soon they were on their way across the causeway.

Now the city was just ahead, looming up in all its legendary beauty. The taxi turned into Piazzale Roma, and stopped near the water. Here there was a crowd of motor boats, the Venetian version of taxi. Sally gave their destination, the Hotel Billioni, and soon they were moving out into the Grand Canal, the huge elegant highway that sliced through the centre of Venice. At last the boat turned into a tiny side canal and halted where a flight of steps came down to the water. The boatman took their bags and led them the few yards to the hotel.

After checking in they were shown upstairs to the two rooms where they were to stay. Sally went straight to the window and threw it open.

Below her the little canal was quiet and mysterious. Darkness was falling and the only light on the water came in soft gleams from the windows above.

The little she had seen of Venice so far was enough to confirm its reputation for romance and mystery. It would attract lovers, perhaps for their honeymoon.

The word 'honeymoon' directed her thoughts to Frank, despite her efforts to prevent it. These days she didn't often let herself think of him, not since she'd resolved to put him out of her life.

He'd attracted her. His kisses had pleased her, yet for some reason she'd resisted his urging to take them further.

'C'mon, Sally,' he'd said, sounding irritated. 'This is the twenty-first century. Kisses aren't enough any more.'

He was right. If she'd wanted to go to bed with him she was free to do so. But something held her back. When she found him with another girl it was hurtful but not really a surprise.

He accused me of being cold, she thought, and maybe he was right. Will I ever want a man so much that I can't control myself? Probably not. If it was going to happen I guess I'd know by now.

She gave a little self-mocking laugh.

I've come to the city of Casanova, but somehow I don't think even he could make me passionate. I'm too sensible. But then, I've always needed to be.

The sound of Charlie moving in the next room reminded her why good sense was necessary. She had made many sacrifices for him. Even being here was a sacrifice, as it might have cost her the chance of a wonderful job. She was an accountant, working independently with reasonable success, but suddenly a job with a major firm beckoned. If she'd stayed at home it might have been hers. But they were unlikely to keep it open for her, at least, not for more than a week.

She could hope, but she knew hope could be destructive if it was all you had.

Charlie's head appeared round the door.

'I'm starving,' he said. 'Let's go and have some supper.'

The restaurant downstairs was humming with life. Delicious smells wafted from the kitchen and they spent a merry few minutes choosing food.

'And this is just the start,' Charlie said. 'We're going to have a great time.'

'You might. My time will be taken up watching you to stop you going crazy.'

'Hah! So you say. But this is the city of Casanova, the great lover. You'll be fighting the men off.'

A chuckle overhead revealed that one of the waitresses had heard and understood.

'It is true,' she said. 'This was the home of Casanova.'

'Never mind him,' Sally said. 'He can wait. I want some supper.'

'Fish,' Charlie enthused. 'Did you ever see so much fish?'

'We have everything you want, *signore*,' the waitress declared.

'It's lucky you all seem to understand English so well,' Sally observed. 'We'd be really lost otherwise.'

'But people come to Venice from all over the world. We must be able to talk with them. Now, what can I get you?'

'I'll have the codfish prepared with olive oil, garlic and parsley.'

'Me too,' Charlie announced.

'*Duo baccala mantecata,*' she announced triumphantly, and bustled away.

'Is that what we ordered?' Charlie asked.

'I guess it must have been.'

'It sounds great. I'm beginning to think you did the right thing in hauling me out here.'

'I didn't haul you.'

'Come on. You practically chucked me into your suitcase.'

'Well, all right. I was getting a bit worried by those phone calls that kept coming from people who wouldn't give their name. One called himself Wilton but the others wouldn't tell.'

'Wilton—well—yes.'

'You mentioned him once, made him sound like a nasty piece of work.'

'Was that the only reason? Didn't you want to get shot of Frank?'

'Frank doesn't exist any more. Don't ever mention him again.'

Charlie gave her a hilarious look.

'First you kick Casanova into the long grass. Then Frank. Perhaps the entire male sex should be nervous about you.'

But he laid a hand on her shoulder in a friendly clasp. Young and self-centred as he was, Charlie could still be sympathetic.

They spent the meal planning the next day's sightseeing.

'We'll get on a *vaporetto*,' she said. 'That's the water equivalent of a bus. That way we'll see the Grand Canal and the great bridges across it. Then we can go and see St Mark's Square.'

'Only it's not a square,' he said, studying a leaflet. 'It's a huge rectangle full of shops and restaurants.'

'It sounds lovely.'

Finally they drifted back upstairs.

'Goodnight,' he said, giving her a peck on the cheek. 'Sleep tight, and be ready to take Venice by storm tomorrow.'

She gave him a gentle thump and left him. Before going to bed she went to the window to enjoy the view over the little canal. Below, she could just make out a small pavement with steps leading down into the water. A man's voice seemed to be coming from inside. He sounded angry.

Suddenly a door was flung open and the man came out. From a little way above Sally could just see that he was tall, dark, in his mid-thirties, with a face that might have been handsome but for the fierce, uncompromising look it bore. He was speaking Italian, which she couldn't understand until he snapped, *'Lei parla come un idiota.'*

I guess I know what that means, she thought. He's calling someone an idiot. Not a guy you'd want to meet on a dark night. He's probably the bouncer.

The man stormed back into the building, slamming the door. Sally closed the window and went to bed.

That night it rained. By morning the rain had stopped, leaving the streets wet and glistening. They spent the day discovering Venice, wandering through narrow alleys that inspired the imaginative side of Charlie's nature.

'All these twists and turns,' he enthused. 'If you were following someone in secret they'd never know you were there. Or if you were trying to avoid them you could dart out of sight often, then dart back again.'

'You're just a naturally tricky character.' She laughed.

'Well, it can come in handy,' he agreed, not at all offended by being called tricky.

They found where to board the *vaporetto* for a trip along the Grand Canal, which was followed by a visit to the Rialto Bridge. Finally they took a water taxi down a narrow canal.

'I will set you down just there, where the canal ends,' the driver said, 'and from there it's just a short walk to St Mark's.'

At last they reached the Piazza St Marco. One end was dominated by a huge, decorative cathedral, while around the sides were dozen of shops and cafés with tables outside.

'Let's sit out here,' she said.

'Wouldn't it be warmer inside?' Charlie protested.

'It's not too cold and I like sitting outside and watching the world go by, especially in a place like this—so many people, so much happening. But you can go inside.'

'And look like a sissy while my sister sits out here?' he asked with a grin. 'No, thank you.'

They found a table and ordered coffee, glancing around them as they sipped it.

'Oh, look,' Sally said suddenly. 'That lovely dog.'

She'd fixed her eyes on a brown and white springer spaniel bouncing around, enjoying the puddles.

'It's so nice to see them having fun,' she said.

'You're a sucker for dogs,' Charlie observed. 'If you love them so much I can't think why you don't have one.'

'Because I'd have to leave him alone so much. It wouldn't be kind. You never knew Jacko, did you?'

'The dog you had before I was born?'

'That's right. I adored him. He had a terrific personality, just like that one over there. Bouncing everywhere, demanding attention.' She struck a dramatic attitude. *'Wuff! Look at me!* That's what he's saying.' She turned to the dog, who had come close enough to hear her. 'Yes, all right, I'm looking at you. You're beautiful.'

His ears perked, his face lit up, and the next moment he was flying towards her, bouncing into her lap, sending her coffee flying over her clothes.

'Hey, look at your jacket!' Charlie exclaimed.

'Oh, heavens! Well, never mind. It's only a jacket. It was my fault for calling him.'

'And he's covered you with wet paw prints.'

Suddenly a scream tore the air. *'Toby! Toby!'*

A young boy was dashing across the piazza towards them, waving his arms and screeching. Just behind him was a middle-aged woman, also running, her face dark with thunder.

'Toby!' the child shrieked. *'Vieni qui!'*

He reached Sally and flung his arms around the dog so fiercely that she was knocked off balance and would have crashed to the ground if Charlie hadn't seized her just in time.

The woman began a tirade in Italian. Without understanding the words Sally gathered that she was furious and her manner towards the animal was alarming.

'It's all right,' Sally said firmly. 'It was an accident, not his fault.'

Hearing her speak English, the woman responded in the same language.

'He's a bad dog,' she said. 'He's never been disciplined properly and it's time something was done about him.'

'No!' the child screamed, tightening his arms around the animal. 'He's not bad.'

'Of course he's bad,' the woman said. *'Signor, mi appello a voi.'*

The man she appealed to seemed to have appeared from nowhere. Looking up, Sally thought she recognised him as the man she'd seen at the hotel the night before. But it had been so dark that she found it hard to be sure.

'Papa!' the little boy screamed.

So this grim, scowling creature was the father of the boy. Only a swift response would help now. She confronted him.

'It's all a misunderstanding,' she said, praying that he spoke English. 'I don't know how much you saw—'

'I saw the dog hurl himself at you and cover you with mud,' he said in a voice that brooked no nonsense.

'He's just affectionate. It was my fault for calling out to him. He was being friendly.'

To her relief he nodded. 'That's generous of you. Thank you. Are you hurt?'

'Not at all. It's not his fault that it's been raining.' She patted the furry head. 'You can't help it raining, can you?'

'*Wuff!*'

'There, you see. He agrees with me.'

The boy gave a chuckle. The man's face relaxed and he laid his hand on the child's shoulder. The only person not pleased was the woman. The man spoke a few words to her in Italian. She glared and walked off.

'She hates Toby,' the boy complained.

'How could anybody hate him?' Sally said. 'He's gorgeous.'

'He makes a mess of the house,' the man said. 'Usually in a place she's just cleaned. Pietro, I think you have an apology to make.'

The child nodded, took a deep breath and faced her, with his arm protectively around Toby. 'We're sorry for what happened, *signorina*.'

'It's all right. Sometimes accidents just happen, one after another.' She leaned down to the dog. 'As long as Toby isn't hurt.'

As if to answer Toby licked her face. In response, she bumped her nose against his. Pietro giggled in delight. Toby promptly licked her again, then turned to Charlie, who received his attention with pleasure.

'While they're occupied, allow me to buy you a coffee,' the man said. 'Then I will escort you back to your hotel. And of course I will pay for your clothes to be cleaned.'

'Thank you.'

'Where are you staying?'

'At the Billioni Hotel.'

'Ah, yes.'

'Actually I think I saw you there last night. You were calling someone an idiot. Are you the manager?'

'I'm the owner.'

'Oh—er—well, it's a very nice hotel.'

'But it still needs some work. You don't have to be tactful.' He offered his hand. 'My name is Damiano Ferrone.'

'I'm Sally Franklin.' They shook hands cordially.

'And the young man with you? Your husband?'

'Goodness no. He's barely grown up. That's Charlie, my brother.'

'And you are here on holiday together?'

'Yes, we decided to explore the world a little. I know most people don't take holidays in January—'

'But Venice is beautiful all the year round. We get many visitors in winter. But perhaps you regret the rain.'

His glance indicated the damp paw marks on her jacket.

'I don't regret anything that lets me meet such a gorgeous dog,' she said. 'I just love them.'

'So I saw. You immediately became my son's favourite person.'

They laughed together. It was remarkable, she thought, how his face, though formed in stern lines, softened when he spoke of the child.

'Does his mother mind the muddy paw marks?' she asked.

'He has no mother. My first wife died giving birth to him nine years ago. He used to have a stepmother but she left us.'

'Doesn't she ever come back to see him?'

'Never.'

'Does he mind? I mean—were they close?'

'Not really, but she was the only mother he'd ever known, so he clung to her. But when our marriage ended—'

A shriek of laughter interrupted them and made them turn to where the others were playing.

'I remember when I had a dog just like that,' she mused. 'Full of vim and wanting to be the centre of attention all the time.'

'He belonged to Pietro's real mother. He's the only legacy he has of her.'

'So of course he treasures him. *Yes, over here!*' She raised her voice as Toby raced back towards her, hurling himself once more into her arms while Pietro jumped up and down with delight. Damiano smiled fondly at the sight of his child's happiness.

'I think Toby is trying to tell you something,' he observed.

'Well, he certainly seems to like me,' she ventured.

'Enough to invite you to our house this evening for dinner—as a way of apologising for ruining your clothes. Please say you'll come.'

Pietro looked up into her face, nodding eagerly, and she guessed he was the one Damiano was trying to please.

'We'd love to come,' she said, 'wouldn't we, Charlie?'

'Sure, fine.'

'I'll just go back to the hotel and change,' she said.

'There's no need,' Damiano declared.

'But look at the mess Toby's left me in,' she

said, comically indicating the paw marks. She put her face close to the dog's. 'This is all your fault.'

'He's very sorry,' Pietro said, 'and he'll make it up to you at dinner. But you must come with us now.' He nudged Toby. 'Tell her she's got to come now.'

'*Wuff!*'

'Well, if Toby commands, I can't refuse.' She laughed.

It was the right answer. Both Pietro and his father beamed. And Sally found herself overtaken by a sense of exhilaration, caused by the sheer unexpectedness of the situation. For someone who spent her life analysing figures and making careful plans there was strange delight in being swept away without warning. When Damiano offered her his arm she took it with pleasure.

From St Mark's Piazza it was a short journey to the water, where they found a taxi that took them along the Grand Canal.

'Is your home far?' she asked.

'You can see it now.'

She gaped at the sight of the building that they were nearing. Knowing he was rich enough to own a hotel, she'd expected a substantial home, but this was huge and elaborate.

'There?' She gasped. 'But it looks like a palace.'

'It's a hotel.'

'Another one of yours?'

'Yes, I own it. I live in the building next door.'

His home was smaller than the hotel but still impressive, with a broad stairway leading up from the great hall to the upper floors, where tall, decorative windows let in the light.

Bustling towards them was the woman who'd been in St Mark's.

'You've met Nora,' he said. 'She runs the house and she'll show you around.'

Sally thought she detected a puzzled look in the housekeeper's eyes, after the way they had met. But she greeted her cordially and showed her to a room on the ground floor.

'You can be comfortable here until dinner is served,' she said. 'There is a bathroom next door.'

The room was magnificent, with furniture that looked antique and expensive. On one wall was a large picture of a woman luxuriously dressed in eighteenth-century clothing. Gold hung around her neck, and much care had clearly been lavished on her appearance.

Probably to impress the man who had paid for it, Sally thought.

'Who is that?' she asked Nora.

'That was the Duchess Araminta Leonese, three hundred years ago,' Nora said with a smile. 'She was a very notable woman. The duke married her in the face of much opposition. His family wanted him to marry an aristocrat, but he said it had to be her and nobody else.'

'Wasn't she an actress?' Charlie said.

'She was a lady of the stage. And in those days—'

'In those days that was a big scandal,' Sally mused.

'Oh, yes. Very big,' Nora agreed.

As she turned to leave Charlie murmured to her, 'I could murder a drink.'

'Follow me, *signore.*'

They departed together.

On the wall was a mirror where Sally could study her appearance. Her jacket was a mess. The clothes beneath it were undamaged but they were plain and frugal, and she felt self-conscious at how they would look in these wealthy surroundings. But then she thrust the thought aside. Everything was happening out of her control, and it was pointless to worry about it.

She went to the window, which had a small balcony overlooking a narrow canal where she could see a gondola making its way along the water. Smiling, she turned back into the room.

Then she froze at the sight that met her eyes.

The figure standing there was small but alarming. It had a monstrous head. Horns reared up from the forehead, the eyes were huge and threatening, and the great nose was more like a beak. This terrifying creature had crept into the room unnoticed, and now stood there in a silent, deadly challenge.

At last it spoke.

'It's only me,' said Pietro.

CHAPTER TWO

FOR A MOMENT Sally couldn't take it in. Her head was spinning too fast to think.

Then the creature removed the alarming mask, revealing Pietro's face.

'It really is you.' She gasped, sitting down suddenly.

She guessed she should have thought of the child when she saw the apparition was so short, but the stunning effect of the face had driven everything else out of her mind.

'Did I make you jump?' he asked.

'Just a little.'

He came close, smiling in a cheeky, friendly way that dispelled the last of her alarm.

'I just wanted to show you my mask,' he said.

'It's—very effective,' she said with feeling.

'Yes, I'm going to wear it for the carnival. Everyone dresses up. I've got several masks but I think this is the best.'

He put it back on, turning the monstrous face towards her with an air of triumph.

'Aaaaaargh!' she cried, throwing up her hands in a theatrical pretence of terror that made him laugh with delight.

'What's going on?' Damiano demanded from the door. 'Pietro, what are you up to? You should know better than to scare our guest twice in one day.'

'Don't worry about me. I'm strong enough for anything,' Sally declared.

'You may need to be if he's going to get up to his tricks.'

'But that's what boys are for, getting up to tricks,' she protested. 'If they behave too well it's no fun.'

'Then I can promise you plenty of fun,' Damiano said with an ironic glance at his son. He pointed to the door. 'Out! And behave yourself, if you know how.'

When Pietro had vanished Sally said, 'If he does know how I bet he'd never admit it to you.'

'That's hitting the nail on the head. I must leave you for a moment to make an urgent phone call, but when you're ready the dining room is just across the hall. They're already laying the table.'

He departed, and a few minutes later Charlie entered, rubbing his hands.

'We've really fallen on our feet,' he said glee-fully.

'Yes, they're lovely people,' she agreed.

'That's not what I meant. This guy has money. We can have a great time here!'

She regarded him wryly. It was clear Charlie's acquisitive side was rearing its head.

'Charlie, I know your idea of a great time,' she said tersely. 'Just try to behave yourself.' A sud-den impulse made her add, 'If you know how.'

'But I don't,' he said with an air of innocence. 'I never have, according to you. And now we're in Venice, you don't expect me to behave myself here, do you?'

'Whatever I was thinking of to bring you to the great pleasure city I can't imagine.'

'You wanted me to have fun, and I'm going to show my appreciation by having the best fun ever.'

'That's what I'm afraid of. Now push off while I make myself ready for the evening.'

'But you haven't brought any extra clothes with you.'

'No, but I can try a little make-up.'

If it would make any difference, she thought, self-mockingly. In this beautiful place she was more than ever aware that her looks were com-monplace.

Many women would have envied her slim figure but she regarded it askance.

A bit too slim? she thought. Thin? Perhaps. Frank used to say he liked me that way, but the creature I saw in his arms had luscious curves and they were all on display. Ah, well! What does it matter now?

She made up as elegantly as possible but she couldn't rid herself of the feeling that the Duchess Araminta on the wall regarded her with disapproval. Nora had hinted that she was a courtesan, a woman who'd spent her life enticing men, and the message she seemed to send out to Sally was, *Is that the best you can do?*

'Yes, it is,' she replied defiantly. 'We can't all be great beauties.'

Soon there was a knock at her door and Pietro presented himself in another mask. This one wasn't alarming, but cheeky, leaving his mouth free. He took her hand and they went to the dining room together, followed by Charlie and Toby.

Supper was a collection of fine Venetian dishes. Damiano was attentive, asking her several times if he could get her anything. She revelled in it, unable to remember when she had last been so spoilt, and determined to enjoy it to the full. She guessed the treat would not last long.

Charlie too was having the time of his life,

plaguing Damiano with questions about things to enjoy in Venice.

'There's plenty to see,' Damiano told him. 'The palaces, the monuments—'

'I meant something a bit livelier than that,' Charlie said. 'Places where things happen and you have fun.'

'There's La Fenice,' Damiano mused. 'I've been there many times myself and always enjoyed it.'

'Do plenty of people go there?' Charlie asked.

'About a thousand every night.'

'Oh, boy, what a place! What do they do when they get there?'

'They sit quietly and watch the performance,' Sally intervened before Charlie could make an even bigger ninny of himself. 'It's an opera house.'

'Opera—? You mean—*serious stuff*?' His tone revealed exactly what he thought of serious stuff.

'Not necessarily,' Damiano said. 'Sometimes they perform comic operas. We might go to see one. I'll arrange it if you like.'

Charlie gulped. 'No need to go to any trouble for me,' he said hastily.

Sally caught Damiano's eye and smothered a laugh. It was clear that he had understood Charlie perfectly, and was enjoying teasing him. His quizzical look asked her if he'd got the situation right. She gave him a brief nod.

'This food's terrific,' Charlie said, with the air of someone changing the subject at all costs.

'I'll tell the cook you said so,' Damiano said. And the moment passed.

Pietro made the evening delightful. He'd taken a shine to Sally after the way she'd defended him and Toby. Especially Toby, who was allowed to stay curled up under the table, from where he could be fed titbits.

'Can you really eat in that mask?' she asked the boy. 'I know it doesn't exactly cover your mouth but it doesn't look comfortable.'

His reply was to bite a sausage, which he only just managed.

'All right,' she laughed. 'I guess I don't understand masks. What does this one make you?'

'A monkey,' Pietro said 'But I've got another one that makes me a mouse.'

'I'd like to see that. But not now,' she added quickly. 'Finish your supper first.'

Giving a quick glance at his father, Pietro replied with a studied air of obedience that didn't fool her for a moment.

'Yes, *signorina*.'

'Oh, please, not *signorina*. My name is Sally, and that's what I like my friends to call me.' She added anxiously, 'We are friends, aren't we?'

Pietro nodded eagerly, and returned to eating. But before long he began chatting again, so that it was hard for anybody else to get a word in edgeways. Occasionally there was a mild protest from his father, but on the whole Damiano seemed inclined to be indulgent. Once he mentioned bedtime, but Pietro's cry of, 'Please, Papa,' was enough to make him retreat. Yet at last even Pietro was unable to hide the fact that he was falling asleep.

'Go along,' said his father. 'Say goodnight.'

'Goodnight, Papa.' Pietro turned to Sally. 'Goodnight, Sally.'

'Goodnight, Pietro. Goodnight, Toby.'

'Will you be coming back to see us again?'

'Yes,' Damiano said at once. 'She will.'

But Pietro's clasp on her hand tightened as though he was still uncertain.

'Look,' she said, 'why don't I come up with you and we'll say goodnight up there?'

He nodded.

'Go on,' Damiano said gently.

He gave his father a brief hug, then seized Sally's hand again. Together they went upstairs.

As soon as she went into Pietro's room she saw two large photographs on the sideboard. Both were of women. One had a beautiful, gentle face. The other was reasonably good-looking, but with a face that was intelligent rather than charming. She guessed these were Damiano's two wives.

When Pietro was in bed she opened her arms. He hugged her enthusiastically before snuggling down.

'You really will come and see us again, won't you?' he asked.

'Yes.'

'Promise?'

'Promise.'

She stayed with him until his eyes closed. Then she kissed his cheek and crept quietly away.

She found the dining room empty. At the far end was an open door that seemed to lure her on. She went to explore and found herself in a room with many windows overlooking the canal. Damiano was there, sitting near a floor-length window that led out onto a small balcony. He made a gesture indicating the chair beside him.

'I hoped you would join me,' he said, raising his wine glass. 'So I came prepared.'

He pointed to a second glass on the table, and began to fill it with rosé wine.

'Later in the year we could sit out there on the balcony,' he said. 'But the forecast is more rain.'

'What's happened to Charlie?' she asked.

'He's in the next room, watching television. There's a good soccer match on. It'll keep him happy for a while.'

Thus leaving them in peace to talk without him. That was the unspoken message, and she was glad of it.

'You really caught him off-guard, talking about opera,' she said.

'Yes, whatever he came to Venice for, it wasn't that.'

'However did you guess?' She chuckled, and he joined in.

'But why did he come here? He strikes me as a bouncy young man who doesn't go in for sight-seeing.'

'True,' she sighed. 'He was getting a bit too bouncy. He's only eighteen and—well—'

'I understand. I've got a younger brother who often makes me tear my hair out. And I wasn't a saint at eighteen either.'

'And now?' she couldn't resist teasing.

'Certainly not! Go on telling me about Charlie.'

'He went a bit too far so I seized him by the scruff of the neck and told him to obey me.'

'Obey you? I thought you said you were his sister, not his mother.'

'That's right, our parents died years ago. In some ways you could say I *am* his mother. He's been in my care since he was eleven.'

'Don't you have any family to help? Uncles, aunts, grandparents—?'

'None. Charlie's the only family I have.'

He frowned.

'Does that mean caring for him has denied you any existence of your own?' he asked. 'No career, nothing?'

'Oh, no, I have a career as an accountant, and now that he's older I can give it more time. At the moment I work freelance, so I can make my own hours, but soon I think I'll have a very good job with a big firm. My interview went well, and I'm crossing my fingers.'

'But is that all you have? You're not married?'

'No.'

'And there's no—forgive me, I don't mean to pry, but surely there's a man at home in England, waiting for you to have the time to marry him?'

'No,' she said wryly, thinking briefly of Frank before consigning him to nothing.

'No emotional life at all?' Damiano mused in a tone that gave nothing away.

'I've had moments, but they didn't amount to anything,' she said, trying to sound casual.

'The men didn't meet your high standards?'

'Or I didn't meet theirs. That's just as likely.'

'So now all the hopes of your life are concentrated on the job?'

'*Signore*—'

'Wait. Enough of that. You told my son that you didn't like formality. Your friends call you Sally. My friends call me Damiano.'

'Damiano,' she mused. 'I don't think I've ever heard that name before.'

'My enemies would tell you it suits me. It comes from the Latin word Damianus, which means to conquer and subdue. It can even mean to kill.'

'Your enemies? Do you have many?'

'A respectable number.'

'Respectable?'

'I'm a businessman. If you don't annoy a few people along the way you're not doing it properly.'

'So you've annoyed enough people to feel proud. You face each other, you conquer and subdue them, and they go off saying, "I'll make Damiano sorry. Damn him!"'

He grinned. 'I see you know how it's done.'

'Do they ever actually manage to make you sorry?'

'Would I admit it if they did?'

'I'm learning all the time. I must remember what you've taught me. It could be useful in my own business life.'

'Here's to you.'

He raised his glass. She raised hers and they clinked.

From below came the sound of singing. Damiano opened the door to the balcony and ushered her out. Now they could see a gondola gliding along the narrow canal below them. A young man and woman sat holding each other, lost in the delight of their love, their surroundings, and the gondolier singing behind them while propelling the boat.

As the song ended he looked up, saw them and called out, 'The world belongs to lovers.'

'Yes,' cried the loving couple. 'Yes, yes.'

They waved upwards, saluting the two on the balcony.

'Oh, dear,' Sally said. 'They think—'

'It happens all the time in this city, especially in winter when lovers come here for the magical peace and quiet. Please don't be offended.'

'I'm not offended,' she said quickly.

There could be no offence, she thought, in being thought the lover of this handsome man. Luckily she was armoured, or she might have been in danger.

'But why did the gondolier say it in English, not Italian?' she asked.

'His passengers must be English. It's intriguing how many tourists come from your country. They seem so cool and restrained on the outside, but Venice brings out another side of them—one they usually prefer to hide, or even didn't know they had.'

As if to prove him right the couple in the gondola were sharing a passionate kiss as they drifted away. Further ahead the little canal broadened out into the Grand Canal, from which came the noise of music and cries of delight. As they watched a *vaporetto* went past, crowded with excited passengers, some of them singing, some cheering.

'It's almost as though Venice has two different personalities,' she said. 'So quiet and gentle at one end of this little stretch of water, so exuberant at the other end.'

'You're right. But it's not just two different personalities. A dozen, perhaps a hundred.' He shepherded her back into the room, adding teasingly, 'Like the English, really.'

'You obviously think you know a lot about the English.'

He showed her back to her chair, and sat beside her. Suddenly he was no longer joking.

'I know I like them,' he said quietly. 'My first wife came from your country, and I see her in Pietro. It's a side of him that I encourage.'

'Is that why he speaks my language?'

'Yes, I've raised him to be bilingual.'

'He must be very bright to speak it so well while he's so young. He's a lovely child.'

'Yes, he is. There's something I want to say to you. Thank you for making him so happy. It means a lot to me to see him laughing and playing as he's done today.'

'Doesn't he do so often?'

'Sometimes he seems merry, but it never lasts

very long. He's haunted by the feeling that two mothers abandoned him. As I mentioned earlier, his real mother died before he could know her. His stepmother simply left him.'

'Poor little soul,' Sally murmured. 'Does she never contact him at all?'

'Never. She said that he would be better off if she was completely out of his life. But it was just for her own convenience, not for Pietro's sake. She never loved him. He has only me.'

'And he's everything to you, isn't he?'

'Yes. Both for his own sake and because—' His voice died.

'Because of his mother?' she urged gently.

He nodded.

'Because of Gina,' he said quietly. 'We had such a little time together. Pietro was born a month prematurely. It killed Gina and the baby himself nearly didn't survive. In her last hours Gina was wild with terror, fearing for him. She had no thought for her own danger, only his. I held her in my arms, begging her not to leave me, but I knew it was useless. She was being snatched away by a power beyond her control, and only her baby mattered. So I swore to her that I would care for him and protect him all the rest of my life. Nothing would matter but his happiness.'

Sally had a strange feeling that the world had changed. Even the universe. This city, which was like nowhere else, might be the answer, but she sensed something more. The man sitting close by, talking in a soft voice, had been known to her for only a few hours. Yet he was confiding in her in a way that said she was not a stranger, but someone to whom he felt close, because that was what he wanted to feel.

She tried to tell herself to be sensible, but common sense had gone into hiding.

'Did your promise comfort her?' she asked.

'I thought so. She whispered, "God bless you," so perhaps it did for a brief moment. Then—she tried to say something else. But she choked and couldn't speak. In her last few moments she was desperate to tell me something, but she died before she could say the words. Now I'll wonder all my days what she wanted to say that was so important.'

'But surely, in your heart you know what it was,' Sally said. 'She wanted to say that she loved you. It couldn't be anything else but that.'

He raised his head and she saw in his eyes a smile that made her heart turn over. There was a warmth in it that felt as though he was reaching out and touching her, enveloping her in some feeling she'd never known before: a feeling that she wanted to know for ever.

'I think,' he said softly, 'that you must be the kindest person in the world.'

'No,' she said, suddenly self-conscious at the strength of her own feelings.

'Don't tell me that you're not kind. I wouldn't believe it.'

'You don't really know me.'

'Yes,' he said. 'I do. I knew you as soon as we met in the Piazza San Marco.'

The air was singing about her ears and she was at a loss for an answer. Part of her had the same feeling, that she knew him as though they had been acquainted for ever. But another part said exactly the opposite: that here was a man of mystery and contradictions; that she might know him all her life, yet never understand the first thing about him.

Somewhere in the back of her mind a voice was whispering that it might be intriguing to follow that path, seeking the man he really was, perhaps finding him, and then—

Abruptly she closed off the thought, wondering what possessed her to give it even a moment. Soon they would say goodbye and he would cease to exist. Which would surely be a good thing.

Her next words seemed to come of their own accord, without any conscious decision.

'You think you know me,' she said, 'but I don't even know myself. I often believe I do, but then I discover I was wrong.'

He smiled.

'Most of us could say the same. I'm convinced you've come to the right place. I promised Pietro that you would visit us again, which was rather impolite of me without asking you first—'

'I forgive you,' she said with a smile. 'You couldn't have asked me first, in front of him.'

'Thank you. You're a lady of great understanding. So when you come for your next visit we'll spend a little time together and—who knows? I may manage to introduce you to yourself.'

There was a hint of teasing in his voice, but also a hint of temptation, leaving her free to choose which one to follow.

But it was an impossible choice; one she didn't feel ready to make.

Her reverie was interrupted by the sound of bells from the clock tower in St Mark's.

'Goodness, is that the time?' she said, checking her watch. 'I had no idea it was so late.'

'Yes, time can slip past when you're thinking of other things,' Damiano agreed quietly.

Suddenly there was a noise overhead. They both tensed with surprise, and looked up to find Pietro looking down at them from an upstairs window.

'Hello,' he said.

'You should be in bed,' Damiano told him in an unsteady voice.

'I wanted to see Sally,' he said cheekily. 'Are

you all right, Sally? Is Papa looking after you properly?'

'He's doing his best,' she said in a voice that was also a little unsteady. 'But it's time I was going home.'

'I'll call my driver,' Damiano said. 'We'll take you back to your hotel.' He took out his cell phone and said a few words in Italian.

'He'll be here in a couple of minutes,' he said when he'd hung up.

Sally raised her head, meaning to say goodbye to Pietro, but to her surprise he'd vanished and his window was closed.

They collected Charlie and the three of them headed for the door, where a surprise awaited them. Pietro stood there, fully dressed.

So that was why he'd backed away from his window so quickly, Sally thought.

'What are you doing here?' Damiano demanded. 'You're supposed to be in bed.'

'But we're going to take Sally home,' Pietro said. 'We're her friends. We should all go with her.'

'Very well,' Damiano conceded, opening the door. As Sally passed him he murmured, 'At least my son has manners. He likes you so much he wants to be the perfect host.'

'Oh, come on,' she chuckled. 'When you were

his age, didn't you seize any chance to stay up late?'

'Yes, I suppose that's it. All right, let's get going.'

He helped her into the motor boat. Charlie and Pietro got in, and they began the journey down the narrow waterway into the Grand Canal. At this time of night it was still brilliantly lit, and music floated towards them from a distance. It felt like drifting through another world.

Part of her regretted leaving at this moment. Part of her was glad. It had been a relief to avoid facing the question that was teasing her. Damiano had spoken of introducing her to her real self. If she'd had to answer him—what would she have said?

She had no idea.

CHAPTER THREE

AT LAST THE Billioni appeared. The boat came to a halt and Damiano helped her out. As they entered the hotel the receptionist became alert and respectful, responding to his gesture indicating that he wanted her complete attention.

So he really is the owner, Sally thought.

Suddenly she heard Charlie mutter, 'Oh, heavens! How did that happen?'

'How did what happen?' she asked, looking around.

Then she saw what had alarmed him. Through an open door she could just see into a room where there was a man whose face she recognised with alarm. He was in his thirties, sloppily dressed, unshaven, with dark hair that looked as though he didn't bother to comb it. She didn't know his name but she'd seen him lurking around their home in England, and knew that he was bad news.

'Charlie, who is he? Charlie? Charlie, where are you?'

But he'd slipped away. Damiano was still engaged in conversation, so she headed for the door to confront the man.

'I've seen you before,' she said. 'In England.'

'Yes, I'm Ken Wilton and I'm looking for that brother of yours. Where is he?'

'Why do you want him?'

'Why do you think? He ran off owing me a lot of money, and I want it now.'

Her worst fears were realised, but she set her chin and faced him.

'Charlie paid all his debts. I know that.'

'You think that,' he sneered. 'I guess you gave him some money, huh?'

'Yes. More than enough to pay what he owed.'

'Is that what he told you? Well, I'm telling you that there's a much bigger debt come to light, and I'm here to collect. Otherwise there'll be trouble. So you'd better go and get him. He knows who I am.'

'I'll do no such thing. I don't believe he owes you anything.'

He moved closer to her.

'Really?' he sneered. 'I wonder just how sure you are of that, and how long it might take to change your mind.'

Sally tried to turn away from him, but he took her arm in a ruthless grip. 'Where's your brother?' he said.

With a great effort she managed to wriggle free but he came after her and struck her, causing her to fall. A sharp pain went through her head as it hit the wall.

She heard a voice screaming, 'Sally! *Sally!*'

Suddenly Pietro was on his knees beside her, trying to take her into his arms. Then a man's voice cried out her name again and Damiano appeared in the doorway. The next moment her attacker had rushed to the window and dived out. They heard a splash as he landed in the water outside.

Damiano dashed to the window, glanced out, then looked back at Sally on the floor. A porter had followed them in, lured by the noise. Damiano barked some orders at him, then came to kneel beside Sally, drawing her up so that his arms supported her.

'What did he do to you?' he groaned.

'He knocked her down,' Pietro wailed. 'I heard him yelling and then he hit her. Oh, Sally, please don't die.'

Tears were pouring down his face. Through her pain and confusion one thing stood out for Sally—Pietro must be protected from the horror of what he'd seen...

'I'm all right, Pietro,' she said. 'Truly. Just a little bump.'

'We'll see what the doctor has to say about

that,' Damiano said. 'I'm taking you home with me. You can't stay here in case that ruffian returns.'

'It's Charlie he's after,' she murmured. *'Charlie—'*

'I'm here,' he said, appearing. 'He's got away. They couldn't catch him.'

'Then the sooner we leave, the better,' Damiano said.

He rose, drawing Sally gently to her feet, then lifting her in his arms.

'Don't worry,' he said. 'You're coming with me and you're going to be safe.'

'He's after Charlie—' she whispered.

'He'll be safe too. You have my word on it. Trust me.'

All her instincts agreed, and she found herself relaxing in his arms as he carried her out, pausing only to bark some more orders at the receptionist.

'They'll pack up your things and send them after us,' he told her.

'My bill—'

'Taken care of. Don't worry about anything.'

Her head was aching and she could do nothing but rest it against his shoulder and yield everything up to him. She felt herself being lowered into the motorboat, Damiano sitting beside her with Charlie and Pietro facing. As they swept away Damiano made another call on his cell phone.

'The doctor will be there when we arrive,' he said when he'd hung up. 'Here.' He handed the phone to Pietro. 'Call Nora, tell her to have two rooms ready.'

Pietro did as he was told. Sally couldn't understand the Italian words, but she sensed the tension in his voice. When he finished he spoke urgently to Sally.

'She's getting everything ready. We're going to look after you.'

'Thank you,' she whispered, reaching out to take his hand. The little boy's concern touched her heart.

As Damiano had said, the doctor was there before them. Damiano carried her upstairs to the room that would be hers, laid her down on the bed, then stood back to watch.

The doctor declared that the bump on her head wasn't serious, but a few days' rest would do her good.

'She'll get everything she wants here,' Damiano said. 'I'd like you to come again tomorrow.'

'Certainly. I brought some painkillers with me, and she should take some now. Then rest and good food is what she needs.'

'She will be all right, won't she?' Pietro asked anxiously. 'She isn't going to die?'

'Definitely not,' the doctor said kindly. 'She just needs to take it easy.'

Pietro gave a brief smile but his air was still one of anxiety. Sally reached for him.

'I'm stronger than I look,' she assured him. 'Don't worry about me.'

His reply was to throw himself into her arms.

'Steady, don't shake her,' Damiano protested.

'It's all right,' she hastened to say. 'He isn't hurting me.'

Nora brought in some water, which Sally used to take the painkillers. Then the men departed while Nora tucked her under the duvet. Whether it was the pills or the shock of the evening's events, Sally began to feel drowsy, and soon the world drifted away.

She awoke to find Damiano sitting by the bed, watching her.

'How are you feeling?' he asked.

'Better. My head isn't hurting. I'm sorry to give you so much trouble.'

'Don't talk nonsense,' he said, speaking with a gentleness that contrasted with his words. 'You are no trouble.' He indicated some bags on the floor. 'Your things have arrived, so you can unpack soon.'

'My bill—'

'I told you not to worry about that. You were attacked in my hotel. That's my responsibility and the least I can do is wipe out your bill, and Charlie's. Don't mention it again.'

'But that man—Wilton—what happened to him?'

'He escaped, which may be a good thing. Otherwise the police would have become involved and you'd have found it distressing. The hotel security staff will find him.'

'But how will they know what he looks like?'

'They'll know his appearance from the camera outside the front door that records the face of every visitor,' Damiano said. 'They'll track him down and persuade him not to trouble you again.'

She didn't ask what 'persuade him' meant. This man would have his own methods of persuasion that would probably make her shudder. She found that she could no longer fight off the horror. Tremors afflicted her, and she clenched her fists, struggling to stay calm.

'Come here,' Damiano said.

The next moment his arms were around her, enfolding her in warmth and comfort.

'It's all right,' he murmured. 'Hold onto me. I'm going to look after you.'

She believed him. The feeling of safety seemed to envelop her, warming her heart and her flesh in a way she had never known before. She clung to him, letting her head rest on his shoulder, wishing it could stay there for ever.

For several minutes neither of them moved. Then he lowered her gently onto the pillow.

'I want to understand everything,' he said. 'Getting rid of that lout was just the start. What else do you need me to do?'

She hesitated, glad to feel his strength and support, but uncertain whether she should tell him any more about Charlie.

'You've done enough—' she began.

'That's for me to say,' he replied in a voice that was quiet but brooked no argument. 'I want to know what lies behind this, and you're going to tell me.'

She sighed.

'I know I'm safe, but Charlie isn't. Wilton was after him, and I don't think he'll give up.'

'I promise you, he will when I've finished with him,' Damiano said.

'Where is Charlie now?'

'Safely settled in the room next to you. Tell me about him. Once before you implied that he's irresponsible, even for his age.'

'He doesn't mean any harm, but he's young and he doesn't think things through. He gambles a lot, and loses.'

'And guess who has to pay up to get him out of trouble,' Damiano said wryly.

'I suppose I shouldn't, but I find it so hard to refuse him.'

'Even though you must know you're not doing him any favours in the long term. He's never going to learn better as long as he gets away with it.'

'I know,' she said wretchedly, 'but there's no one to protect him, and that's my fault.'

'I don't believe that. Stop putting yourself down.'

'Seven years ago I was knocked down in the road. My parents set out to drive to the hospital. A lorry crashed into their car and they both died.'

'And you blame yourself for that?' he demanded. 'Surely it wasn't your fault that you were injured?'

'No, but if it hadn't been for me they wouldn't have been on the road and an eleven-year-old boy wouldn't have been left an orphan. Since then I've been the only family he has.'

'How old were you at the time?'

'Twenty-one.'

'Just twenty-one, and your life was taken away from you.'

'No—no, not really. People expect to make sacrifices for the ones they love.'

'But they don't expect to live in a prison. Isn't that your life? Behind bars, with Charlie's needs holding the key?'

It was true. She'd never faced it before, but Damiano saw everything.

'But you're the same,' she said. 'You build your life around Pietro's needs.'

'A father expects to do that for his son. But a sister is entitled to a life of her own. One day he'll have grown up enough to go his own way, and you'll be left stranded in a desert. No husband, no lover, no children.'

'But I have my career. I'll always have that. When he finally leaves me I won't be in that desert.'

'You will if your career is all you have.'

'But what can I do? He needs me, but I can't make him understand. I beg him to be careful, and responsible, but he just thinks I'm making a fuss about nothing.'

'As lads of that age often do,' he agreed.

'I can't just abandon him.'

'But can you defend him? When men like that come calling can you drive them off?'

She shook her head. 'No, I guess I can't.' She gave him an ironic smile. 'If you ever want a job as a bodyguard I've got a vacancy.'

'I'll remember that,' he said, returning the smile. 'But when you return to England, and Wilton pursues you again—'

'Don't, don't!' she cried. 'My head's spinning. I don't know which way to turn.'

'Perhaps fate will show you.'

She shook her head. 'That's a nice thought, but

you can't rely on fate. You have to fix things for yourself. Only I don't know how.'

'But perhaps fate does know how. Just be patient and see what happens. Now it's time for you to eat something. Nora has prepared you a meal, and Pietro is going to bring it in. He's determined to stay awake and be one of your attendants. You won't mind having him fuss over you, will you?'

'No, of course not. It was terrible for him to see what happened. I know it upset him, and if looking after me helps him cope with it, I'll be very glad.'

'Thank you. I knew you'd understand.'

The door opened a crack and Charlie's face appeared. 'Can I come in?'

He came to the bed and hugged her. 'Sorry, sis. I just seem to land you in it, don't I?'

'Don't flatter yourself,' she told him in the chivvying tone she often used with him. 'There's nothing about you that I can't cope with.'

'I'm sorry. If it wasn't for me—'

'If it wasn't for you I'd be lonely. Don't blame yourself, Charlie.'

'Perhaps I should. Perhaps you should just dump me—'

'And leave you at that man's mercy? Get real. Grow up. We're going to do this my way.'

He gave a comically theatrical salute. 'Yes, ma'am, no, ma'am, three bags full, ma'am.'

She tried to mimic the salute, and winced at the pain in her arm.

'No more of that,' Damiano said. 'You've got to rest every part of you until you're better.'

'That's right,' Charlie said.

He gave her an uneasy smile, which she returned. It was true, as she'd told Damiano, that Charlie was spoilt and self-indulgent. But his nicer side had a disconcerting habit of asserting itself unexpectedly. As he grew more mature, she thought, that side would be even more in evidence.

'I'll leave you,' Charlie said. 'Take care.'

He kissed her and went to the door. As he opened it they saw Pietro standing there with a plate in his hand. He advanced to the bed and set the plate on a small table.

Nora was there too, with a tray, but this was Pietro's moment and she stayed in the background.

'Are you better?' he asked anxiously.

'I'm fine.'

'Truly? *Truly?*'

'I promise. Oh, that food looks lovely.'

But as she took the first bite she went, *'Ouch!'*

'What's the matter?' Damiano demanded quickly.

'My mouth, where he hit it. It's just a bit sensitive. I shall have to eat carefully.'

Luckily the food was soft and she managed

well. Pietro didn't take his eyes off her, and she had a sad awareness of how painful this must be for him, given his history.

While she ate Nora unpacked her bags and put the contents in a chest of drawers. Then Pietro and Nora left them.

'Is that all you can eat?' Damiano asked.

'Yes, it's lovely but I can't manage any more.'

He removed the tray and sat close to her on the bed.

'Get some sleep,' he commanded. 'Don't lie awake worrying.'

He wrapped his arms about her, giving her a sweet feeling of being enveloped in warmth and peace. Looking up, she saw his face more gentle and kind than ever before. His lips were barely an inch from hers as he whispered softly, 'I'm your friend and you can trust me. Don't forget. That's an order.'

She gave a weak laugh. 'I guess it's an order I'll have to obey.'

He nodded, and for a moment she thought his mouth would touch hers. She held her breath, uncertain whether she wanted the kiss or not. But in a second it would happen, and she would know.

But his lips brushed hers so softly that she barely felt them.

'I'm sorry, I shouldn't have done that,' he murmured. 'Did I hurt your mouth?'

'No, you didn't hurt me,' she whispered.

'Goodnight, Sally. We can talk again tomorrow.'

'Yes—tomorrow—'

'You'll feel better then. Your mind will be clearer. But in the meantime, remember you have nothing to worry about. Both you and Charlie are under my care. Trust me.'

She watched as he left and closed the door. Then she closed her eyes, wondering what was happening to her.

She had a mysterious feeling of having been transported into a different universe, one in which nothing was certain and everything was mysterious.

She wondered how she could ever cope in such a place. For many years now she'd valued certainty above all else. It had started in her childhood when, without quite knowing why, she'd known that she was a disappointment to her parents.

Then Charlie was born, and she'd begun to understand. Their joy over having a son had shown her that a daughter would always be second best.

She'd struggled for their attention by plunging into her school work, using her natural gift for figures to get to the top of the class. They had praised her, but she'd always known in her heart that Charlie came first.

Some sisters would have blamed and resented him, but her natural generosity shielded her from bitterness. Plus even as a small child Charlie had a wicked charm that won her over. He was naughty, cheeky, impertinent. He could make her tear her hair out. But his giggle could win her over.

Their parents' death had made him her responsibility. She'd applied herself to the task with an earnestness that had caused arguments. Charlie was shocked to find her stricter than his parents, and blamed her for it.

'You think all life is about figures,' he'd accused her from the authority of thirteen. 'If the sums add up you think the world's OK.'

She hadn't known how to tell him that her severity was based on apprehension. She dreaded to let him down. If she was sometimes too stern, wasn't that better than being too easy-going and seeing him get into trouble?

And she recognised that his accusation was partly right. There was a certainty about figures that made her feel safe.

Yet now she found herself in a world where nothing was as expected. Surprises bounced out to confront her every moment, and certainty barely existed.

But she would cope. She was efficient, organised, strong; virtues that had carried her through life thus far. What could possibly happen here that could defeat her?

From outside came the sound of singing again. Moving carefully she eased herself out of bed and went to look out. There below was another gondola with another romantic couple. And there too was Damiano sitting on the balcony, looking over the water.

After watching him for a moment she drew back, closed her window and leaned against it, her heart beating.

Next morning Nora was all attentiveness, bringing her breakfast, waiting on her, making sure that she took her pills. Charlie looked in, then Damiano, and Pietro. The little boy looked pleased to see her in good spirits, and hugged her.

'I've got to go to school now,' he said with a yawn. 'But you'll still be here when I get back, won't you?'

'Definitely she will,' Damiano said. 'Come on, I'll walk you to school.'

'You don't need to,' Pietro said. 'I can go alone.'

'Well, perhaps—'

'I'm not a little kid, Papa.'

To Sally's surprise he seemed grumpy and offended, unlike the sweet-natured child she was beginning to know. Perhaps 'macho' set in early, she thought.

Pietro vanished without waiting for further argument, and she met Damiano's eyes.

'He's getting independent,' she said.

'I guess so. He certainly doesn't like me going to school with him. I was afraid he might be falling behind but his teachers all say he's very bright and works hard, so I'm not sure why I'm suddenly unwelcome.'

'Is it a long journey, difficult, dangerous?'

'No, it's just a few alleys away. Venice isn't like any other city where you have to cross roads and be afraid of cars. He can manage it alone, but now and then I like to go with him. I hoped he liked it too, but recently he's started saying no.'

'He's turning into his own man. You heard what he said. He's not a little kid.'

'I'd have thought he was still a kid, at only nine, but—well—'

'He's going to be like his father,' she said in a faintly teasing voice. 'When he grows up he'll insist on doing things his way.'

'I'm not sure that being like me would be a blessing,' he said wryly.

'That depends exactly what you mean.'

'I mean a lot that I'm not willing to explain. Now, about today. I want you to stay in bed. The doctor will come later, and we'll see what he says. In the meantime, you stay here.'

'But what about Charlie?'

'Leave Charlie to me. I'll be in the hotel next door and I'm taking him with me. I'm planning some changes, a small theatre, a casino. He might have useful suggestions.'

'So he'll be safely under your wing,' she said. 'Thank you.'

'Don't worry about anything. Goodbye for now. I'll send some English newspapers up if you need distraction.'

He was as good as his word. She spent the day browsing the papers, eating, sometimes nodding off. The doctor called and said she was improving enough to get up the next day.

Once she got out of bed and went to the window where, by a lucky chance, she saw Damiano and Charlie in the alley below, deep in conversation.

He's safe, she thought contentedly. Oh, thank goodness we found this man.

She returned to bed and dozed for another hour. When she awoke there was a soft knock on the door.

'Come in,' she called.

It was Pietro, carrying a mug.

'English tea,' he said proudly. 'Careful!'

The last word was directed at Toby, who came flying into the room and leapt on the bed, forcing Pietro to back away to protect the tea.

'It's all right, I've got him,' she said, clutching

Toby. With an unconvincing attempt at severity she added, 'You pestiferous pup. You can't stop hurling yourself at me.'

'Pestiferous?' Pietro queried, setting the tea down beside her. 'Is that an English word?'

'Yes. It has several meanings, but one of them is "annoying".'

'Ah! *Irritante*.'

'Definitely.' She wagged a finger at Toby. 'You are *irritante*.'

'Wuff!' He licked her finger.

'He just takes everything in his stride.' She laughed.

'He does with you, because he loves you.'

'And I love him. Oh, yes!' She put her arms around the dog. 'He reminds me of my own lovely Jacko.'

'You have a dog?'

'I used to, a few years ago. He died. But he'll always be with me because we were so close. He was the first one who really loved me.'

He stared. 'Didn't your parents love you?'

'Yes, in their way, but—I think having a girl was a big disappointment for them.'

'But that's not fair,' Pietro said indignantly.

'Life often isn't fair,' she said wryly. 'Some things we just have to put up with. Anyway, when they finally had a son the family was complete.

And I always had Jacko to turn to. He belonged to my father, but he and I were specially close.

'One day I walked into the room and Jacko's whole face lit up with delight at the sight of me. Nobody had ever reacted to me like that before, and I just had to love him. I could tell him things I couldn't tell anyone else.'

Pietro nodded. 'Yes. They understand everything.'

'I'm sure you talk to Toby a lot.' In a teasing voice she added, 'Does he give you good advice?'

'No, but he listens.'

There was a forlorn note in his voice that made her reach out to him, touching him gently on the shoulder.

'What is it, Pietro? Are you unhappy?'

He didn't answer, but she could see confusion in his face, and guessed he wasn't sure whether to confide in her.

'Can't you tell me?' she asked softly. 'I'm a good listener. Almost as good as Toby.'

He smiled, clearly reassured by her understanding, but still unwilling to speak.

'Tell me,' she urged. 'Please, tell me.'

CHAPTER FOUR

When Pietro still didn't reply she said, 'Won't you trust me? You never know, I might be able to help.'

But he shook his head. 'Nobody can help. You can't change things that have happened.'

'That's true. But you can change what you do about them. Is there something wrong at school? I remember when I was at school there was often something wrong. I kept getting into scrapes.'

She sensed at once that she was succeeding. Pietro's intake of breath and his astonished look told her she'd hit a bull's eye.

'It's school, isn't it?' she asked gently. 'What happens?'

'They laugh at me,' he said morosely.

'Why?'

'Because of *her*, and the way she ran off.'

'Her? You mean your stepmother?'

'Yes, *her*. It was the school concert. I was going to sing a song all on my own. She and Papa were going to be there, but she didn't come. He told me that she'd gone away.'

Sally drew a sharp breath. 'You hadn't known she was leaving?'

'No. She was at home when I went to school that day, but she didn't come to the concert. Papa was there. He thought she was coming, but she didn't. Her seat stayed empty, and they laughed at me.'

'Who did?'

'The others in my class. They thought it was funny to see me look silly. Especially Renzo. The rest of them admire him, and if he laughs they all laugh.'

The class bully, Sally thought wryly. I've met a few.

'But surely he's not still laughing?' she ventured.

'He keeps finding new things to jeer at. He says I must be a monster if my mother had to run away from me.'

'Have you told your father about this?'

'No, *no!*' he shouted in sudden agitation. 'He mustn't know.'

'But why not?'

'I can't tell him everyone thinks I'm an idiot.'

'But he'd be on your side. He wouldn't let them bully you.'

'I'd look like a weakling. Papa only likes strong

people. Promise you won't tell him.' He reached out and clung to her, crying, 'Promise, promise.'

Horrified by his misery, she put her arms about him, holding him in an embrace that she hoped he would find comforting. His request tormented her. How could she deceive Damiano about his child's unhappiness? Yet how could she deny Pietro a promise for which he begged so desperately? In despair she raised her head.

And then she saw Damiano.

He was standing in the open door, his gaze fixed on them, his expression astounded. Instinctively she raised a hand and waved him away. Without hesitation he backed off.

'Promise,' Pietro said again, looking up at her.

'All right, I promise. I think your father should know, but you're the person to tell him.'

'No,' he said. 'I can't. He'd just think I was stupid.'

He drew away from her, his face set as though he was pulling himself together, determined to deny a moment of weakness.

'I'm going,' he said. 'Don't forget your tea.'

'I won't. Thank you, Pietro. You've been very kind.'

He left without another word. Sally listened, wondering if he would discover his father in the corridor. But she heard nothing, and after a mo-

ment Damiano appeared. He closed the door behind him and stood staring at her.

She knew a moment's pity for the misery in
his face. This was a man who'd received a cruel
blow, and was reeling from the shock.

'Did Pietro see you?' she asked anxiously.

'No, I kept out of sight. Can you imagine that?
I hid from my young son. I was afraid to let him
see me. What a coward!'

'You're not a coward. If he'd seen you he'd
have been upset. It's not cowardly to consider
your child's feelings.'

'Thank you, but I can't give myself that escape.
I didn't do it for his feelings, but my own. If he'd
known I was there listening he'd have hated me.'

'Sit down,' she said, patting the bed. 'We need
to talk.'

He sat, moving so heavily that it was almost a
collapse, and dropping his head into his hands.

'I had no idea!' he groaned. 'I never dreamed—'

'You heard what he said?'

'Every word.'

'But you always knew he was upset at his stepmother's departure.'

'Yes, but not the way it happened, vanishing
on the night he was looking forward to.'

'You never suspected she was going?'

'No, she was cunning enough to keep quiet. I
spent the morning at work and went to the school

from there. We were supposed to meet at the concert. When she didn't show up I just thought she'd been delayed, but when we got home there was a letter saying she'd left.'

'And nothing for Pietro?'

'Nothing. Not a word, not a parting gift. Nothing. One of the neighbours looked in and saw what was happening. She had a son at the same school and I imagine that's how the story got around. But I never knew about the trouble it has caused Pietro.'

He raised his head, looking at her with despairing eyes.

'Why didn't he tell me? He must know I love him.'

'But he wants your respect as well. He's afraid to seem weak.'

'At his age? He's a child.'

'When you were his age did you think of yourself as a child?'

'No,' he groaned. 'In his position I'd have been too proud to ask for help, just like him. Of course he couldn't tell me. But he could tell you. I saw the way he threw himself into your arms, the only person he could trust. I heard him beg you not to tell me—'

'Don't blame him for that,' she said quickly.

'I don't blame him. I blame myself for being a father he can't talk to.'

He dropped his head back into his hands. 'What can I do? I just don't know where to begin.'

Saddened by his self-blame, she reached out to him. At the feel of her gentle touch he leaned sideways until his head was nearly against her shoulder. It was so like the moment when Pietro had sought refuge in her arms that she drew a tremulous breath at the strange sensation that fluttered through her without warning.

Suddenly the stern, commanding man and the vulnerable child seemed almost the same person.

But he pulled away quickly, as though alarmed by what he was doing. He thumped a knee with his fist, not looking at her.

'I think I know how you can deal with this,' she said. 'Talk to him about your own childhood. I'm sure he confided in me because I told him I used to have problems when I was at school. That made him feel I could understand. Try to tell him about something that put you at a disadvantage when you were a child, so that you felt you couldn't cope. Then he'll realise that you know how he feels now, and he's more likely to confide in you.'

He considered for a moment before nodding. 'I see what you mean. But I can't remember—'

'Can't remember ever being at a disadvantage?' she asked. 'You'll think of something. And if you don't, then invent something.'

'Lie?'

'Yes. Sometimes lying is the best thing to do. It can be the most useful, the kindest, and the most honest.'

He gave a wry grin.

'Thank goodness you're here. I can see I'm going to need your advice. You won't be leaving yet, will you? The longer you're here, the better.'

'Yes, I'll stay a while. I don't want to go back to England in case Wilton finds us again.'

'Right. You're better off here. And I've promised to protect Charlie.'

'Thank you.'

He rose and went to leave, pausing at the door.

'Tell me something. You promised Pietro not to tell me what he'd confided in you. If I hadn't overheard, would you have kept that promise?'

'I'd have kept it for a while, so that I might persuade him to tell you himself.'

'And if he didn't? Would you have told me?'

She hesitated.

'You wouldn't, would you?' he persisted.

'I don't know. He's suffering this terrible feeling of betrayal by your wife. To break my promise would be to betray him again. I simply don't know what I'd do.'

'That's what I thought,' he said wryly. And departed without another word.

She drank her tea slowly, trying to get her mind

around the events of the day, not entirely succeeding.

I've got to get up, she thought. I'm too helpless here, and helpless is something I can't afford to be.

Before she could move there was a knock on her door and Charlie came in.

'Nora wants to know if you'll have dinner up here or come downstairs,' he said.

'I'm coming down.'

'I'll go and tell her.'

'Wait, Charlie, there's something I want to ask you. How did Wilton know where you were?'

'He knows a private detective. He owes Wilton money too, and he pays it by chasing the rest of us.'

'So they were watching you. That's scary. What will happen now?'

'Nothing, Damiano's sorting it. He's got friends in high places who'll see that Wilton is booted out of the country. He's probably gone already, and he won't be allowed back. Damiano's a powerful man, Sally. We're lucky we've got him on our side.'

'Yes,' she murmured. 'We are. I dread to think what might happen if—'

'If what?'

'Nothing,' she said quickly. This was no time

to start speculating on how life would be if she and Damiano were on opposing sides.

'But what were you going to say?' Charlie demanded.

'I forget. But I wanted to ask you why Wilton said you still owed him money.'

'Oh, just a bit.'

'How large a bit?'

'Well—'

'You don't even know, do you?' she demanded.

'I'll have to work it out. I was going to pay him later, when I had a bit more—you know—'

'And when would you have had any more?'

'I could get a job.'

'How many times have I heard you say that? Oh, heavens! Now I've got to find some more money.'

'It's all right. Damiano's going to sort that too.'

'You think we can leave everything to him?'

'But that's what he said. "Leave it all to me." And if he's willing to help us, why not take it?'

Why not? she thought. Because a small inner voice warned her to be cautious about Damiano. He was a man used to being in control, giving orders and seeing them obeyed.

Except where Pietro was concerned. For his son's sake he had put himself in her hands, frankly admitting his need of her help.

She remembered him asking if she would have

kept her promise to the child, and his tense expression when she'd said she didn't know. There had been a hint of defiance in her answer, and she guessed defiance was something he wasn't used to.

So he's not completely in control, she mused. Some control is in my hands. And he knows it. He doesn't like it, but he loves Pietro enough to accept it.

'Tell them I'll be down in a moment,' she said.

She dressed quickly, and hurried down to find Damiano in his office. He smiled at the sight of her.

'Nice to see you looking well.'

'I'm feeling fine, and I'm very hungry.'

'That's a good sign.'

'But I also wanted to talk to you. Charlie told me what you said to him, about helping him with his debts. I'm sorry all this got dumped on you. We had no right—'

'It's not a matter of rights,' he said. 'It's a matter of helping my friends. After all, you're helping me.'

'Yes, but I don't want you to think I'm taking advantage, making use of you. Charlie's debts are my responsibility, not yours.'

'But I can help out for a while. Are you upset because I'm interfering?'

'I don't know what I am,' she admitted. 'Confused, yes. Scared, yes. But I won't dump it all on you. I don't expect you to clear the debts he owes.'

Before her eyes Damiano's 'mask' changed. The efficient organiser vanished to be replaced by a humorous charmer. It was there in the gleam of his eyes, and even more in his words.

'All right, we'll make a deal,' he said. 'I'll take care of Charlie's debts, and I won't worry about what it costs me, because at the end I'll present you with a bill.'

'You'll—?'

'It'll probably be a very large bill because I'll add interest for my trouble. But it'll save you the problem of being indebted to me, which I know will make you happy. It will, won't it?' His expression was teasing.

'B-but of course,' she stammered. 'What else—?'

'If you could only see your face now. Sally, you can't have thought I meant it about the bill?' Damiano smiled.

'But—'

'I was just trying to show you how absurd you're being.'

'But it feels as though you are taking control and—'

'And you prefer to be the one in control,' he supplied.

Since this was exactly what she'd been thinking about him it made her speechless for a moment. But then she saw that he was still smiling, and sighed.

'You're right,' she admitted. 'It's just that—'

'It's just that you didn't choose for it to be this way, but having to look after Charlie forced you.'

'I guess it made me a bossy woman.'

'Don't worry. To show that I forgive you I'll halve the bill.'

'Oh, really. Well, I may present you with one myself. Twice as large.'

'Hey, you're learning. But like I said, I believe in paying my debts, and as a start I'm going to spend some time introducing you to Venice. You're going to love it.'

'I know I will.'

'We'll start tomorrow.'

He was as good as his word. Next day, Pietro had a day off from school, so they all set out after breakfast in a motor boat driven by his personal driver.

'Anything special you want to see?' he enquired.

'I've heard the Calle Malipiero is very interesting,' Charlie declared with a fair assumption of lofty authority.

Sally gave him a questioning glance, which Damiano met with a grin. Silently he mouthed, 'Casanova.'

'Of course,' she murmured.

After that Pietro spoke up, directing them to the places he thought of as fun, until Damiano took them all for lunch in a restaurant.

'Time to go home,' he said at last.

'Yes, we must get back to Toby,' Sally said. 'He'll be wondering where we are.'

'I told him,' Pietro said. 'He understands.'

Sally shook her head. 'Some dogs never understand being left alone.'

Pietro nodded, and it seemed she was right, for Toby greeted their return with yelps of joy, hurling himself at Pietro and then at Sally.

'He likes you.' Pietro laughed. 'He's saying that you're one of us.'

'Yes,' Damiano said. 'She is.'

But she could never be one of them, she thought wistfully. Soon this lovely time would be over, leaving her only with happy memories. But she would enjoy it while it lasted. Then she must return to reality, and the job on which her future hopes rested.

'Can I ask a favour?' she said to Damiano.

'Anything.'

'I need to send some emails from my laptop—'

'No problem. I'll connect you to my Internet.'

Suddenly there was a squeak of excitement from Pietro.

'Uncle Mario!'

A young man had appeared in the hall, beaming as he opened his arms to the child who flung himself into them.

Damiano had mentioned a younger brother, and from their similar features Sally guessed this must be him. The two men embraced and exchanged greetings in Italian.

'You'll have to speak English for a while,' Damiano said, bringing him to her. 'We have an English guest. Sally, this is my brother, Mario. Mario, this is Signorina Sally Franklin. She's Pietro's new best friend.' A *wuff* from below made him add, 'And Toby's.'

Mario chuckled and shook Sally's hand vigorously. 'I'm honoured, *signorina*.' His eyes looked her up and down and his smile was full of appreciation.

'How come you're here so soon?' Damiano asked.

'The job ended a few days early,' Mario said, speaking in a cautious way that showed he was choosing the words carefully. 'So I seized the chance to dump myself on you.'

'Get settled in and then we can talk.'

While Mario went upstairs Damiano explained, 'He's a journalist. He lives in Rome but he travels around a lot and his latest job brought him near here. So we planned for him to visit me. Nice to see him early. Now, let me have your laptop.'

He connected her quickly and skilfully, then vanished to give her privacy. She spent an hour in touch with England, but there was no sign of news about the job. After a while a delicious odour coming from the kitchen made her go down to investigate.

'You must teach me how to make that,' she told Nora.

'And you must teach me some English recipes. Oh, dear!'

'What is it?'

Nora pointed to a table where Sally could see a typed envelope.

'Signor Ferrone was here a few minutes ago. He had that in his hand and must have forgotten it.'

'Give it to me.'

Taking the letter, Sally crossed the hall and went down the short corridor to Damiano's room, which the open door revealed to be empty. She entered and went to his desk, meaning to leave the envelope there.

Then something made her stop and stare.

Everything in this room spoke of reserve, calm, unemotional efficiency. Except for one thing.

There on the desk was a photograph of a woman whom Sally recognised from one of the pictures she'd seen in Pietro's room. It was the same person but a different photograph. Pietro's had been laughing and cheerful. This woman's face was almost melancholy, but beautiful, tender. Somewhere deep in those large eyes was a hint of promise.

Damiano had married her for that promise, Sally thought. But she had been snatched from him before it could be more than partly fulfilled. She'd given him their child, then abandoned him to loneliness, There was no memento of his second wife. Only this picture, positioned so that the man sitting at the desk could see it whenever he happened to glance up.

'Can I help you?'

Damiano's voice from the door made her jump.

'I'm sorry, I only came in to give you this.' She waved the envelope. 'I wasn't trying to pry.'

He took the envelope and glanced at the photograph.

'That's Pietro's mother,' he said.

'She was beautiful.'

'Yes, she was. Before she married me she had ambitions to be a model in England. She never made it big but it was looking hopeful. Then she gave it up for me.'

There was a softening in his voice that she'd heard once before when he spoke of Pietro, the son he shared with this woman. His face too was altered, so much more gentle than before that he might have been another man. Or wearing another mask.

How sad, she thought, that Gina hadn't survived to enjoy life with this man. He would have adored her, treated her with generosity and self-sacrifice. She would have been the luckiest woman in the world.

'Poor Pietro,' she said. 'Never to have known her at all. And poor Gina, to have had such a wonderful son and not have known him.'

She heard a sound like the soft drawing of breath, and looked up to find Damiano gazing at her as though something had struck him.

'Yes,' he murmured. 'Yes. You say it so perfectly. Her loss was as great as his.'

'And yours. All those years of happy marriage you would have had, that were taken from you. But also taken from her. She had such a gorgeous little boy, and she'll never know.'

'She does know,' Damiano said quietly. 'I tell her all the time.'

'You—?'

'Thank you for bringing me the letter,' he said, speaking with the fierce energy of a man determined to change the subject. 'It was careless of me to leave it behind. Now, about plans for this evening—'

She went along with his suggestions, speaking mechanically while she tried to come to terms with what she'd just learned. Gina was so real to Damiano, so much still a part of his life, that he talked to her.

How lucky to have won the love of such a man, she thought. How unlucky to have been torn from him so soon.

'So what do you think of that idea?' Damiano asked.

'I—what?'

'We spend tonight in. I want to get Mario talking, to find out why he's arrived early. What mischief has he been up to?'

'You told me your brother often made you tear you hair out. Is he—?'

'Yes, he's the one. He's a bit of a madcap, and it's hard for me to blame him because he says he's just following in my footsteps.'

'I remember you saying you weren't a saint when you were younger.' She added lightly, 'But then, what man is? And think how boring if you were!'

'Ah! A woman of great understanding. Yes, Mario, what is it?' His brother had appeared in the doorway.

'Supper's ready. Nora's about to serve and I'm dying of hunger.'

'Fine. Let's go.'

Was she only imagining his relief at bringing this scene to an end? He had told her something she guessed he'd told few people. She sensed that one part of him wanted to confide in her, but another part backed off. And he was torn between the two.

She had to admit that she too was undecided whether she would have liked to remain here for a while, to see which side of him won. But that could never be. She would be gone soon, and the question would always tease her.

Mario's arrival was a gain. Pietro liked his cheery uncle, and Charlie, perhaps sensing a fellow madman, was instantly at home with him. They were both ardent soccer followers, and spent most of the meal comparing English and Italian teams.

But when supper was over and everyone had settled in the next room, Mario contrived to take the seat beside her on the sofa, saying cheekily, 'You don't mind if I force myself on you, do you?'

'I think I can just about bear it,' she said.

'Good, because I need you to tell me something. Why is my brother so suspicious of me? Just because I turned up a few days early, does he have to think the worst?'

'Shouldn't he?'

'Well, I must admit I fouled up a little. I opened my big mouth once too often. But now I'm here, I'm glad. Otherwise we might not have met.' His glance was admiring.

'Yes, I'm glad we met, too,' she said.

'You are?' he murmured hopefully.

'You're just the kind of friend Charlie needs.'

'Ah, yes, Charlie. Nice lad.'

'Why did you assume that Damiano disapproves of you?'

'Because he always has. I suppose I can't blame him. It's part of being an older brother, and he's made such a big success of his life that he expects the same of me. But he conducts his business hell for leather. Everything has to be the way he wants, and I can't match that.'

'Are hotels his only business?'

'Hotels and other property. He inherited a small fortune from his mother and he turned it into a huge fortune very fast.'

'By buying and selling property in Venice?'

'And Rome, Florence, Milan. I can't complain. The fact is we're only half-brothers. We had the same father but different mothers. That's why he inherited and I didn't. But he was decent. He gave me a share. Then he invested it for me and I profited. I'm not rolling in it but I can afford to be stupid.'

'Lucky you,' she said, laughing. 'That sounds like one of the definitions of happiness. To be stupid without having to fear the consequences.'

'Right. You said it. Damiano's a great guy, and I like his properties, especially the hotels.'

'Yes, I've seen the Billioni. We were staying there.'

'That's one of his minor properties. The main one is the Palazzo Leonese next door.'

So he was an even more notable man than she'd suspected, Sally mused.

She became aware of a nose sniffing at her knee.

'Toby's come to say goodnight to you,' Pietro said. 'He's hurt because you haven't made a fuss of him tonight. That's Uncle Mario's fault.'

'Well, I don't want Toby to be hurt,' she said, enfolding the dog in a hug. 'I'm sorry, Toby. Can you forgive me?'

Wuff!

'And tomorrow we'll play games together.'

Wuff! Wuff!

'And maybe I can play too,' Mario said.

Wuff! Wuff! Wuff!

A spirit of mischief made her wag her finger at the dog and exclaim, 'You mustn't say things like that about Uncle Mario.'

'It wouldn't be the first time,' Mario said. 'Toby doesn't approve of me.'

'Does anybody?' Damiano called ironically from the other side of the room.

They all laughed and Sally saw that Damiano was enjoying the scene. His smile spoke of pleasure, contentment, satisfaction. She met his eyes, and could almost have sworn that he nodded before glancing at Pietro and saying, 'Bedtime.'

'Papa!'

'Bedtime.'

'No argument,' Sally teased. 'You should always obey your papa without question, as I'm sure you do.'

'That'll be the day.' Damiano grinned. 'Off you go.'

Sally went upstairs with him to say goodnight. On returning she found Charlie and Mario deep in a 'lads' conversation. Clearly she wasn't needed in that budding friendship. Right now she wanted to have another talk with Damiano. But once in the hall she could hear him talking on the phone in his office.

She suppressed an irrational feeling of disappointment that he'd forgotten her so soon. She was curious to know more about him, but if she couldn't talk there was another way. She returned to her room, opened her laptop, went online to a research tool, and typed in Damiano Ferrone.

The photograph showed him standing with arms folded, glaring into the camera. The text described the man of property, determined, uncompromising.

There was a list of the places he owned, including the Palazzo Leonese. Logging into its website, she found that it really was a palace, having once belonged to a duke who'd fallen on hard times and been forced to sell it. Now it was a hotel of luxury and magnificence, with its own theatre, ballroom, and a great hall that was licensed for weddings. Every year the Leonese hosted an extensive list of carnival celebrations, including several masked balls.

The sound of laughter floating up from below made her look out of her window in time to see Charlie and Mario walking away along the alley.

Kindred spirits, she thought. At least Charlie will have a friend there to keep an eye on him. This could be a good place for both of us.

CHAPTER FIVE

SALLY SOON FOUND that Mario was a practised flirt, handsome, charming, not lost for words, as his approach to her demonstrated.

'How come I was lucky enough to meet you here?' he asked as he seated himself next to her at breakfast.

'Charlie and I had an accident and your brother was kind enough to invite us here for a few days.'

'A few weeks, I hope,' he said, regarding her significantly.

'Sally is teaching me better English,' Pietro said. 'I know lots and lots of long words.'

'I'll bet you don't know any,' Mario teased.

At once Pietro pointed a finger at him, declaring, 'You are *pestiferous*.'

Mario roared with laughter. 'How on earth did you teach him that?' he asked Sally.

'Through Toby,' she replied. 'He was bouncing around all over me, so I called him pestiferous, but I think the short version might be better.'

'Short version?' Pietro asked instantly.

'Pesky. It suits Toby.' She pointed to where the dog was curled up under the table. 'You are a pesky pup.'

'But he's not a pup,' Pietro protested. 'He's ten years old.'

'Only on the outside,' Sally said. 'Inside he's as daft as he was when he was a baby. Some men are like that too.'

'Pesky, pesky,' Pietro yelled in delight. 'Toby, you are pesky!'

'So are you,' Mario said, rubbing his ears. 'Sally, I can see Pietro is going to learn a great deal from you.'

'Yes, she's got the soul of a school mistress.' Charlie sighed theatrically. 'You should hear how often she calls me a twerp.'

'Twerp?' Pietro echoed. 'What's that?'

'It's a word they won't teach you at school,' Mario said, grinning. 'I've only heard it once before, and that was from a lady who was annoyed because I—yes, well, never mind.'

'But what does it mean?' Pietro demanded of Sally.

'A twerp is someone who is not only foolish but insignificant,' she said. 'Is there an Italian word for insignificant?'

'*Insignificante,*' Damiano said, with a grin at his brother.

'That's right,' Mario agreed. He raised his glass. 'Here's to pesky twerps.'

Raising her glass with the others, Sally caught Damiano's eye. He was gazing right at her, and it seemed to her that he raised his glass higher in her direction, and mouthed, 'Thank you.'

She smiled, saluting him back and mouthing, 'My pleasure.'

After that the mood was merry. The talk turned to Carnival, due to start in a few days.

'Then we have two weeks of fun,' Mario said, 'and it ends just before Lent.'

'And Lent is when people are expected to be virtuous and restrained,' Sally recalled.

'Right. So people really let rip in Carnival, because it'll be so long before they can let rip again.'

'I want to go with Uncle Mario to buy some masks,' Pietro said.

'Ah, yes, you have so few, haven't you?' Damiano said.

'I've worn them all before,' Pietro protested. 'I want to be somebody different, grown up. I'm tired of being just a kid.'

'Why don't you come with us?' Mario asked Sally and Charlie. 'You'll have a great time.'

'Sounds terrific,' Charlie said. 'Count me in.'

'And me,' Sally said at once.

'Perhaps you should rest another day,' Charlie said. 'You don't want to overdo it too soon.'

'I'll be fine,' she assured him.

Her smile told Charlie that if he thought she was going to take her watchful eyes off him while he went on a spending spree, he was mistaken. He made a wry face, accepting the warning.

'So, as soon as breakfast is over, off we go,' Mario said teasingly.

'Oh, no!' Pietro protested. 'I want to come too but I have to go to school.'

'Then we can leave it until this afternoon,' Sally said.

Everyone agreed and the meal finished cheerfully. When it was over Damiano followed her out into the hall.

'You're planning something, aren't you?' he said.

'Me being such a conniving character, you mean? Well, I will admit I have a secret motive. I'll collect Pietro from school this afternoon and—well, it'll give me a chance to form an impression about what's going on.'

'Shouldn't I be there?'

'What do you think?'

'I'm waiting for you to tell me what to think,' he said wryly.

'Thus encouraging me to be more of a bossy woman than I am already,' she suggested.

He laid his hand over hers. 'I'll take that risk.'

'Then don't come to the school. I'll tell you what I find and we'll work towards the next step.'

'Whatever you say,' he replied with an air of submission that didn't fool her for a moment.

'But you could still come to the shop with us,' she said.

'I don't think so. I have enough different selves without confusing the issue with more.' He added in a low voice, 'But I'll be intrigued to see yours.'

'I doubt if I'll buy anything. I'm sure I'll enjoy Carnival, but I don't think I need to dress up for it.'

He shook his head. 'You won't stick to that, Sally. You won't be able to, once you've seen the range of disguises and all the new personalities they offer you.'

'We'll have to wait and see who's right,' she said.

'I'm always right,' he declared. But his teasing eyes robbed the words of bullying.

'So am I,' she said.

'Good for you. We obviously have a lot in common. I recall you telling me, the first evening, that you didn't really know yourself. Sometimes you thought you did, but you were always wrong.'

'Yes. I feel as though I'm a lot of different people. It's something to do with being an actress.'

'I thought you said you were an accountant.'

'I am. The acting is amateur. Just a hobby. I prize it because it gives me freedom.'

'The freedom to be someone else,' he said slowly.

'That's right. It can be boring being the same person all the time.'

'And how many people do you want to be?'

'It changes. It's as though there are two or three versions of me. The accountant has to be severe and sensible, but I have an inner self who secretly wants to go mad and behave wildly.'

'Only secretly?'

'Well, I must admit she gets an outing now and then. I feel as though I'm always wearing a mask. I'm so practical on the surface, but if people knew me inside they'd get a shock.'

'Then you've come to the right place. Venice is a city of many masks. You must find the one that suits you. Or perhaps several that suit you.'

'I suppose we wear different masks for different people,' she mused.

'And some please us better than others.'

Inspiration dawned. 'And when we know which ones please us best, then we know who we really are.'

He nodded. 'I was about to say exactly the same. How well we understand each other. Now I must say goodbye and get to work. Enjoy yourself.'

He went to his office, turning at the door to give her a smile. She answered it with another, and was about to go upstairs when she heard the sound of vigorous voices coming from the break-fast room. Returning, she found find Pietro and Mario deep in argument. Pietro was clutching Toby's lead.

'He wants a mask too,' Pietro declared. 'I promised him one. We could come home and collect him when school's finished.'

'You can't bring him to the shop,' Mario protested. 'They won't let him in. Not after what he did last time. Now give him to me and be off to school.'

Reluctantly Pietro departed.

'I hate refusing him anything,' Mario said. 'I always feel so sorry for him after what Imelda did, running out on him. Do you know about her?'

'She was Pietro's stepmother? I know she abandoned him.'

'She was a monster. In the end she took herself off with a man.'

'She was unfaithful to Damiano?'

'Oh, yes. And not just once.'

'Did he know?'

'Yes. I thought he'd throw her out and divorce her, but he didn't, for Pietro's sake. She was nice to Pietro to begin with because she knew that was the way to get close to Damiano. And it worked. He thought she was nice, and they ended up in bed. But don't tell him I told you that.'

'I promise.'

'Next thing she said she was pregnant. She knew how to get him to marry her and it worked. But there was no baby. After the wedding she said she'd "made a mistake". She'd got what she wanted by then and she thought that was enough.'

'But she was wrong?'

Mario looked around to check that they were still alone. When he spoke it was in a low voice.

'He's only ever loved one woman, and that was Gina.'

'But she's been dead for years,' Sally protested. 'Surely—?'

'Yes, you might think he'd move on to someone else, but he hasn't. Somehow he just can't. I asked him about it once. He'd been drinking or I wouldn't have dared, but he was in a mood to talk. He said he could never love again because once you'd known perfection, nothing else could do. Next day he didn't remember saying anything and I didn't remind him.

'Imelda played the mother for a while, trying to impress him. But she was always jealous of Gina. That became jealousy of Pietro because he's Gina's son. She was sharp with him, neglected him, and finally abandoned him. Damiano was so furious that instead of divorcing her he had the marriage annulled. It was like he wiped her out of existence. That's how he deals with people who offend him. They shrink to nothing and end up wishing they'd never offended him.'

'Yes,' she murmured. 'I can imagine.'

Midway through the afternoon Sally, Charlie and Mario set out on their expedition.

'Pietro's school isn't far,' Mario said. 'Just a few alleys further. They should be coming out by now.'

Out of sight Sally crossed her fingers, hoping that all would be well with Pietro.

She knew her prayers had been answered when she saw him at the school gate, beaming and waving to her. A little distance away, a small crowd of boys was regarding him wryly, almost nervously.

'That's Renzo,' he said, pointing to one in the front.

Renzo seemed about the same age as Pietro, with a lean, scowling face.

'Why is he looking so cross?' she asked.

'Because I got the better of him,' Pietro said happily.

'How?'

'I called him a pesky twerp. He didn't know what it meant, but one of the others did, and they thought it was funny that he didn't know. They started chanting it and it made him look silly.'

'Well done,' she said. 'That's the way to deal with bullies.'

As they left Pietro waved at the little crowd, most of whom waved back. Renzo didn't, but nobody seemed so impressed by him now.

In a merry mood they all made their way along the narrow alleys until they reached the shop that offered dazzling masks and glittering costumes.

Sally had read that Carnival dated back to the twelfth century, when the Venetians fought back against an enemy who tried to conquer them. They were successful, and celebrated their triumph by dancing in St Mark's Square. For the next few hundred years the festival grew until Venice was conquered by another opponent who outlawed Carnival and forbade the wearing of masks.

'That's one reason masks are so important,' Mario told her. 'Our conquerors were afraid of them because having our faces covered made it easy for us to fight back. If you can hide who you are you have great freedom to defend yourself.'

'Freedom to be who you really are,' she murmured.

'If you know who you really are,' Mario observed. 'Maybe you use the freedom to make that discovery.'

'And your enemies didn't want you to know that,' she said.

'Right. In the end they resorted to banning Carnival entirely, and it stayed banned until it was restored nearly forty years ago. The cynics will say it was brought back to attract tourists, but there's more to it than that. Carnival is our proof of liberty, our assertion that we are Venetians.'

Excited, she plunged into exploring the shop. Each mask seemed to offer her the chance to become a new personality, and their sheer number left her stunned.

'I can't get my head around this,' she said. 'How many masks can I buy?'

'First you need a half-mask, to emphasise your beauty,' he said.

She almost replied, 'Beauty? What beauty?' But she stayed silent and was glad when she saw what he'd chosen. It was a half-mask, covering only her eyes, nose and upper cheeks, leaving her mouth free. Flowers and feathers adorned the crown.

She regarded the vision in the mirror with wonder. Truly that was a beautiful woman looking back at her, but was it really herself?

She removed the mask reluctantly, and looked around the shop until she saw something that made her grow still.

'Those white faces,' she said. 'So many, all exactly the same.'

He lifted one. It was a full face mask, completely white except for the closed mouth that was painted on. The only spaces were for the eyes.

'A mask like this has two names,' Mario explained. 'One is *"volto"* which is Italian for "face". The other is *"larva",* which is Latin, and means "ghost".'

'Oh, yes, I can see why,' she said, examining it in delight. 'There's no life in it. It could be a dead person.'

'They're popular because they give nothing away about whoever's wearing them. And that can be useful if you don't want to be recognised.'

He said the last words with a teasing significance that made her look up quickly.

'Don't want to—? Just what do you think I'm going to get up to?'

'Much the same as everyone else gets up to. Don't be offended.'

'I'm not. But watch it, cheeky.'

'Yes, ma'am.'

He grinned, regarding her with pleasure. When she put the beautiful half-mask back on her face he eyed her with frank admiration. But then an impulse made her remove it and put on the ghost mask. Just as the glamorous one gave her a new self, the 'ghost' concealed her entire self.

'I'll have them both,' she said.

Charlie and Pietro were going through the shop excitedly. Pietro chose an extravagant mask with a huge nose. Charlie purchased two masks and two costumes. Sally paid for them, then indicated the door.

'Out.'

'But I also want—'

'Out.'

'Bully.'

'All women are bullies,' Mario said cheerfully. 'The trick is to know how to get on their right side.'

He winked at Sally as he spoke, and she laughed. She liked Mario's jokey nature. Damiano had hinted that he was also a bit of a 'bad lad', but he had so much charm it was easy to ignore everything else.

'Are you going to buy a costume?' he asked. 'Damiano's giving a ball at the hotel to mark the start of Carnival. Say you'll come with me. Come on, say it.'

'All right. It sounds nice. What kind of costume do I need?'

'Just a long dress. It can be anything you like.'

She found what she needed almost at once. It was blue, a slim, satin dress with a long skirt that started immediately under the bosom.

'Makes me look like a Regency heroine,' she mused, pleased with its austere elegance.

That evening Mario and Pietro displayed their masks at dinner.

'That?' Damiano exclaimed, staring at the mask, so ugly that it was practically a gargoyle. 'Isn't that a bit overdone for you?'

'It might have been yesterday,' Sally explained. 'But today it shows the new Pietro, the hero of the hour.'

Damiano regarded his son, noting the air of triumph that had rarely been there before.

'Tell me more,' he said. 'Did you fight a lion?'

'No, he fought a bully,' Sally said. 'Not with fists but with words, which are far more effective. There's a boy at school who's been giving him trouble, but after the way Pietro stood up to him today he's going to be a lot more careful.'

Nothing in Damiano's expression revealed that he'd heard any part of this story before.

'What kind of trouble?' he asked his son.

'Renzo laughed at me,' Pietro said, happy to tell his father everything now that he could boast of a triumph. 'So the others laughed at me as well. But today I called him a pesky twerp. His English is all right in class, but he doesn't understand slang.'

'Pietro caught him off guard,' Sally said. 'That's the way to deal with a foe.'

'Yes, it is,' Damiano agreed.

Across the table Sally gave him a significant glance, urging him to make the most of this chance. He seemed to understand because he went on,

'This Renzo fellow sounds like a few I met when I was your age. Making them look silly is the best way to bring them down. Well done, my son. I'm proud of you.'

Pietro didn't reply in words, but the look he turned on Damiano said everything that was needed. To have won his father's pride and respect filled him with a joy and awe that made his eyes shine. In his turn Damiano too seemed struck by feelings that had taken him pleasantly by surprise.

'I think I'll have an early night,' Sally said. 'I still need a little rest. Goodnight, everyone.'

She slipped away into the hall, feeling that father and son would do better without her intrusion. But before she reached the stairs she heard Damiano's voice behind her.

'Sally, wait!'

Turning, she saw him hurrying across the floor. As he caught her he laid a hand on her arm as though afraid she would escape. He was beaming.

'Is there anything you can't do?' he demanded. 'I was going out of my mind trying to think of a way to put things right for Pietro, but you just waved your magic wand and solved every problem.'

'Not entirely. Renzo will pull himself together and try again.'

'But Pietro will cope, because of your help.'

'And yours. Did you see his face when you praised him? You took a huge step forward with him tonight.'

'Thanks to you. But why did you leave just now? It's your achievement. You must take the credit for it.'

'No, I mustn't. This is about you and Pietro. Not me. Time for me to withdraw.'

'Withdraw? You mean go back to England?' he asked sharply.

'No, I mean… You and that lovely boy have a chance to move on, and I'll just be in the way.'

'But you will return to England eventually,' he mused.

'Is that your way of telling me not to stay here too long?' she asked in a teasing voice.

'No, it definitely isn't. The longer you stay, the better.'

'You'll be offering me a job next.'

He regarded her. 'Maybe I will.'

'You think I'd make a good governess?'

He regarded her in silence for a moment before saying slowly, 'I think you'd be good at whatever you set your mind to.'

'Very kind. I'm flattered. Now I'm going to bed and you should get back to Pietro because I'm sure he's got a lot to say to you. And you've probably got a lot to say to him.'

'I said you were good at whatever you put your mind to, and you've just proved it.'

'Go back to Pietro,' she repeated. 'And don't say I'm turning into a nag because I know I am. It's a very useful accomplishment.'

He smiled. 'I'm sure it's one you use whenever it suits you.'

'I do anything I want when it suits me. Don't you?'

'Absolutely. Goodnight, my dear friend.'

'Goodnight,' she said and hurried away up the stairs. Something in the warmth and charm of his smile had made it urgently necessary to get away from him.

At the corner she looked back to find him in the same place. Now the smile had gone and his face was transformed by a frown that suggested deep inner confusion.

Impossible, she thought. This man was never confused by anything. Yet that strange look stayed with her as she lay awake that night.

The next day, Damiano said, 'Sally, everyone else has shown me their masks. What about you?'

'Don't show him, Sally,' Mario said. 'Take him by surprise.'

'Right, I will.'

'That's the spirit.' He laid a finger over his lips and his eyes twinkled.

'You can't keep it to yourself for ever,' Damiano observed. 'We're having a masked ball in the hotel tonight. I expect to see you there.'

'She will be,' Mario said, slipping an arm around Sally's waist. 'She's already promised to let me escort her.'

'Indeed,' Damiano observed wryly. 'I wonder how you managed to extort that promise.'

'I used my charm, of course. How else?'

'Is that what you call it?' Sally queried with wide-eyed innocence.

'Just tell me if you want protection from my brother,' Damiano told her.

'Thank you but I'm more than capable of taking care of myself,' she said cheerfully.

'Can I come to the ball?' Pietro asked with delight.

'Just for an hour,' Damiano told him. 'Then it will be bedtime.'

'I'm really looking forward to this,' Sally said.

It was true. New vistas were opening before her, and she was advancing to them eagerly. She spent the next few hours preparing her appearance.

Now she found that there was substance in the theory of masks and different selves. The glamorous dress, the extravagant mask with its feathers and jewels surely had nothing to do with her. Yet they attached themselves to her as though this were where they belonged, and she wore them with ease. The only part of herself that could be seen was her mouth, and suddenly this became the mouth of a beauty.

She smiled to herself.

'I don't know who you are,' she murmured. 'But you're me and I'm you. And I think we're going to get on very well.'

There was a knock on the door.

'It's me,' Mario called.

She found him dressed in an elegant velvet suit of dark brown. His face was half covered by a mask that suggested a lion.

'Grrr!' he said, raising his hands with the fingers curled like claws.

'You're really scary.' She chuckled.

'To everyone but you, I hope.'

'Oh, I'm not easily scared.'

'I guess that's why you handle Damiano so well. He scares everyone else.'

'He wouldn't be the perfect employer, would he?'

'Employer? Has he offered you a job?'

'He dropped a hint that I might make a good governess for Pietro.'

'Governess? He's mad. Mind you, he tends to see everything from Pietro's angle. But don't let him get away with it.'

'I won't. But tonight I'm just going to enjoy myself.'

'That's the spirit. Let's go.'

Damiano and Charlie were waiting for them downstairs. Damiano wore an elegant eighteenth-century-tyle black velvet costume. Pietro, dressed as a flamboyant monster, joined them and paraded his new self with glee.

'Come on,' Sally told him. 'Let's show you off.'

Taking his hand, she led him to the kitchen where Nora and the maids greeted him with cries of delight. The men watched them go.

'Wow!' Mario said in a soft voice full of admiration.

'Wow?' Charlie queried.

'Wow!' Mario repeated, still watching Sally's retreating figure. When she'd vanished he regarded Charlie with a touch of unease.

'You really are her brother, right?'

'Right.'

'So you and she aren't—you know—a couple?'

'Are you kidding me?' Charlie exclaimed. 'Even if she wasn't my sister I wouldn't be chasing her. She makes me nervous.'

'Why? She's fantastic.'

'She's a businesswoman. Her life revolves around figures. She makes sensible decisions.'

'Is it a crime to be sensible?' Damiano asked.

'Depends on what she's being sensible about,' Charlie said.

'So what is it with her and guys?' Mario said.

'She's suspicious of guys, always thinks the worst and treats them accordingly.' He grinned. 'So if you're thinking what I'm thinking you're thinking, don't say I didn't warn you. She's a tough cookie.'

'But not with everyone, surely?' Mario protested.

Charlie grimaced. 'There was this guy—I'm not sure what happened. They got close then broke up. I think she found him with someone else, so that made her even more "sensible". I've actually heard her say that real love doesn't exist and romance is just pathetic nonsense.'

'I've said that myself a few times. Most guys have.'

'Sure, but how many women have you heard say it?'

'True.' A smile overtook Mario's face. 'That could even be a challenge.'

A noise from the kitchen announced that Sally was returning, led by Pietro, clutching her hand. Laughing, Charlie went to meet them. When he was out of earshot Damiano observed, 'And you could never resist a challenge, I recall.'

'Some challenges are more interesting than others. There's something extra there, something fascinating,' Mario replied.

'Just be careful,' Damiano advised. 'I think she'd be too much for you.'

'How do you know?'

'I know you.'

'But you don't know her. Not if you see her as a governess.'

'Is that what she told you?' Damiano asked sharply.

'She said you'd hinted about employing her for Pietro. And you do want her to stick around, don't you?'

'Not like that,' Damiano said quietly. He raised his voice. 'Are we ready to go, everyone?'

CHAPTER SIX

THE ENTRANCE TO the hotel was through a private door in Damiano's study. From here a walk along a short corridor took them to the ballroom where the doors were thrown open and cheers greeted them.

The great room was dazzling, full of dramatic costumes and masks that presumably concealed human beings, although for a wild moment Sally couldn't be sure. There could be any number of ghostly beings behind those weird faces. She tried to order her sensible side to take control, but that part of her mind was dancing away somewhere, singing that this was no time for boring good sense.

Mario seized her in his arms, whirling her merrily about the floor. He was a good dancer and she found herself moving more skilfully than ever before. She wasn't short of partners. Several of Mario's friends appeared, demanding to be introduced, then asking her to dance. The one person who didn't approach her was Damiano.

'He doesn't dance much at these evenings,' Mario told her. 'He has duties to perform, which leave little time for his guests. That's his excuse, anyway.'

As he spoke they waltzed past Damiano, who was watching them carefully. Mario waved. Damiano responded with a brief nod, but no more, which Sally found disappointing. He'd spoken so often of his gratitude for her help. The least he could do was give her some attention. As the waltz finished she saw him engaged in an argument with Pietro and went to join them.

'I said you could stay for an hour, and then go to bed,' Damiano was saying.

'I don't want to go,' the little boy said crossly.

'But you need plenty of sleep to be at your best for Carnival,' Sally told him. 'Think of all the fun you'll miss if you can't stay awake. Come on. Let's go.'

Without further argument he took her hand and they slipped out of the ballroom, returning to the house. Damiano came with them as far as the stairs, then he stopped, struck by the sound of singing and laughter coming from outside.

'Someone's having a good time,' he observed, heading for the window.

In the canal outside they saw several gondolas gliding through the water.

'You haven't been in a gondola, have you?' he asked Sally.

'No, and I really look forward to my first time.'

'There's no time like the present. Pietro, can you ask Nora to help you to get ready for bed so that I can take Sally on a trip?'

She half expected the boy to become rebellious again, but he nodded eagerly, evidently liking the sight of them going off together.

'But shouldn't you go back to the ball?' she asked Damiano.

'I've done my duty. Now I'm going to please myself.'

Pietro clearly approved, for he hugged her before dashing upstairs.

'One moment,' Damiano said, going into his office. He emerged a moment later with a heavy jacket that he put around her shoulders.

'I don't want you catching cold,' he said. 'This way.'

'Will we be able to find a gondolier?'

'My own man has instructions to keep himself available for me.'

Clearly the man had obeyed instructions for she saw the vacant boat as soon as they left the building. Damiano helped her in, and when they were both safely seated the gondola began to move.

First they glided out into the Grand Canal,

filled with life and light despite the lateness of the hour. The city was humming with anticipation of the good time to come. Music and laughter were everywhere, and Sally raised her eyes to the starlit sky, revelling in an experience more delightful than she had ever known.

She was unaware of Damiano watching her with a thoughtful look in his eyes. Things had happened over the last few days that had stopped him in his tracks, bringing him to the edge of a decision he'd never thought to take. This very evening the sight of her twirling in his brother's arms had warned him that a crisis could be approaching.

As they passed under the Rialto Bridge she gave a happy sigh and settled back, feeling his arm about her shoulder.

'I envy you,' Damiano said. 'Discovering Venice for the first time is an experience never to be forgotten.'

'Oh, yes,' she sighed. 'I'll have to leave soon, but I'll come back here often.'

He said nothing.

Now St Mark's was growing near. The gondola turned into the side canal that led to the hotel. As they gradually approached Damiano said quietly, 'Are you sure you will leave?'

'I really must get back to my work.'

'But why, when you have a new life opening to you here?'

'Do I? I don't understand how.'

They had reached the steps where they would land. The gondola came to a halt. He helped her out, drawing her down the little side alley.

'Do you really not understand?' he asked. 'Haven't you sensed how much Pietro needs you? You've become so important to him. Will you desert him?'

'No, of course I'll stay in touch from England. I'll write to him often, especially at Christmas and birthdays. I'll come and visit. You might even bring him to visit me.'

'That's not enough. He wants you as his mother.'

'But I'm not his mother.'

He stopped and faced her. 'You could be— if we married.'

Astounded, Sally stared at Damiano, not sure if she'd really heard what she'd thought. He was watching her intently.

She drew a shaky breath. 'That's a very bad joke.'

'I'm not joking. My son has lost two mothers. If he loses you as well he'll be shattered.'

'Then why did you let him get so close to me?'

'Let him? I couldn't have stopped him. It was always out of my hands. I understood that when I went to your room that day and found him in your arms. He'd gone there as a refuge because he knew instinctively that you were who he wanted. And what you've done for him since, giving him the courage and knowledge to face up to that school bully—and showing me how I could make contact with him. I didn't plan it, Sally. Once you'd discovered the way, it was in your hands, not mine.'

'But marriage—I don't believe what I'm hearing.'

'I know it sounds incredible when we've known each other such a little time. But sometimes a little time is enough. We got to know each other and things happened between us. I realised that you fitted in here perfectly. Not just with Pietro but with me. You know what I'm saying. You and I have an instinctive understanding. It's there whenever we talk. When I realised that, I knew you were perfect for my needs.'

'Your needs,' she echoed.

'And Pietro's.'

'Is anyone else allowed to have needs? Don't I have any?'

'Yes, you need a life that isn't dominated by fear for Charlie. And you know I can give you that. He'll stay here with us and work for me. That way I can keep a protective eye on him all the time.'

'But—do you realise what you're saying? You're planning to take over all of my life—'

'That's what happens when people marry.'

'In normal marriages it's mutual, but you're not going to let me take over your life, are you?'

To her surprise he paused to consider before answering.

'Probably not,' he said at last. 'At least, not consciously. But you're such a clever woman that you might do it without my suspecting. One day I'll probably wake up and realise just how much control you've taken.'

'If that ever happened you'd be livid.'

'Maybe. Maybe not. It would depend on your methods.'

'No, stop this. You're trying to get into my head and twist it around.'

'I'm not inside your head, Sally. But I hope I will be one day. I think I might be intrigued by what I find there.'

He was teasing her because he guessed it was the best way to catch her off-guard. Which meant it was just another form of control from a man who was master of all forms. He guessed she couldn't cope with him in this mood and he was perilously close to being right.

But warning bells were sounding in her head. This man had almost everything a woman could need. He was sexually attractive, and he had plenty of charm when it suited him to display it. But she wasn't going to fall victim to feelings that might make her helpless. She stepped backed from him.

'Sally—'

'No. I mean it. I'm flattered by the offer but I'm not something you can just take over to suit yourself.'

He reached for her but she fended him off and turned to walk away.

Damiano watched her, trying to control his inner turmoil. At this moment Charlie's words came back to him.

Her life revolves around figures. She makes sensible decisions... She's suspicious of guys, always thinks the worst and treats them accordingly... I've actually heard her say that real love doesn't exist and romance is just pathetic nonsense.

He sensed that the lad's opinion of his sister, immature though it might be, held a grain of truth. It would have been a mistake to discuss feelings, even if he'd been sure of what his feelings were.

He had a dismaying sense that he'd gone about this proposal the wrong way. But what was the right way? He wished he could be sure.

'Sally,' he called. 'Come back.'

Slowly she turned and made her way back to

him. But then she saw something that filled her with dismay.

Pietro was watching them.

He was standing on the balcony of his bedroom, staring as though frozen by what he saw. Even in the poor light Sally could make out the dismay on his face and his air of tension.

'Oh, no,' she breathed.

Damiano drew a sharp breath and spoke in a low voice. 'He's afraid we're quarrelling. He can't bear the sight, after what he's witnessed in the past.'

'You mean—?'

'Imelda. There were some nasty scenes and he saw too much. I don't want to hurt him.' He took gentle hold of her. 'Don't push me away. Just come close to me.'

She did so, and saw in his face a tension that matched his son's.

'Smile,' he urged.

'Surely he won't see it in this light?'

'You're right. We must do something that he can see.' He put his arms right round her, drawing her close. 'Rest your head on my chest,' he murmured.

She let her head droop against him, contriving to look up in Pietro's direction. He was still there watching, and she wondered if it was only her imagination that he was more relaxed at seeing them at ease with each other.

'Put your arms around me,' he whispered urgently. 'We've got to look convincing.'

She did so, trying to stay in control although her head was spinning. She could feel the beat of his heart against her cheek. It was fierce, like her own, turning the whole world into mystery and confusion.

She wanted to escape, wrench herself from his arms and flee back to a place she understood, where she still had some command of her life. But at the same time she wanted to stay here for ever and never escape.

The warmth of his arms about her was sweet and comforting. How had she ever been angry with him?

'Can you still see Pietro?' he murmured.

She managed to glance up. 'Yes, he's still there, still watching us.'

'Look at me,' he whispered.

She did so and found his lips close to her own.

'He must feel happy about us,' he said softly, his breath whispering against her face. 'Help me, Sally. Help me make him happy. Say you agree.'

'But—'

'Say it. For his sake.'

'All right. I agree.'

Slowly Damiano dropped his head until his

mouth brushed hers. It wasn't a passionate kiss, just a gesture to reassure the child. She held herself steady, waiting for it to be over, feeling the tremors go through her, fighting every instinct that urged her to press against him and tempt him on—and on—

His lips parted from hers, but she could still feel the warmth of his breath. She drew away slowly, glancing upwards at Pietro. He was gone.

She tried to force her mind to take control. Damiano's kiss had a power over her that she must fight. But her flesh challenged her, telling her mind that thoughts were irrelevant. The only thing that mattered was the sweetness flooding through her, destroying the common sense that had always ruled her life.

'No,' she murmured. *'No.'*

'You agreed,' he reminded her.

'I agreed to help you make Pietro happy, but not with marriage. Stop trying to back me into a corner.'

'Say yes. Say yes.'

'I've given you my answer.'

His eyes told her that he'd felt her tremble in his arms and knew his power over her. Now nothing could ever be the same. He would force on her a kiss of passion that would leave her no choice. She braced herself, part fearful, part furious, part craving.

'All right,' he said. 'You need time to think, and perhaps so do I.'

'What—what did you say?'

'This is a big decision and you can't make it all in a moment. You're a businesswoman so you'll need to balance all the pros and cons. We'll talk again later.'

The shock of his withdrawal was so great that her head spun. Her defences had been in place against the passion she was sure he would cynically try to rouse in her. Instead he was turning away, leaving her in a desert. She could have hit him.

While she was still struggling, a drop of rain struck her, causing the vibrant atmosphere to collapse and her confusion to increase.

'Let's go in,' he said, drawing her towards the door of the house.

She'd half expected to find Pietro there, eager to see more. But there was no sign of him.

'Tactful of him,' Damiano said. 'He's left us alone so that he doesn't interrupt—whatever we're planning.'

She ought to leave Venice, she thought. She couldn't bear to hurt the child, but it was better for him not to indulge in groundless hopes. But another voice spoke within her, urging her to marry Damiano and put her whole heart and soul into winning his love.

'You saw Pietro's face,' Damiano persisted. 'Think what it would do to him to lose you.'

'I know, I know,' she said desperately. 'You want to do the best for him, but how can you be sure? What about your second marriage? Wasn't that for Pietro's sake? But it didn't work, did it?'

'That was a terrible mistake,' he said. 'I made a bad choice, but I've watched you with Pietro and I know he's happy with you. You'll transform his life. In return I will protect your brother.'

'Charlie's growing up,' she protested. 'He'll soon be able to defend himself.'

'Soon? Like in about ten years? If he stays here with us I'll give him a job and make sure someone is always watching over him. He'll live with us, and be safe. Can you make him safe in any other way?'

'No,' she whispered. 'I can't, but—but can we base a marriage on that alone?'

There was a challenge in his eyes, silently reminding her how she'd trembled in his arms.

'We can make it work—if we want to. I give you my word that I'll be faithful. If I make a bargain I keep it to the limit. No wriggling out of it.'

'A good businessman,' she murmured.

'It's amazing how often the rules of good business work well in life,' he said. 'You're an accountant—you should know that as well as I do. If someone is reliable and trustworthy when handling your financial affairs they'll be reliable and trustworthy in other ways too.'

Part of her was pulling back, but another part was ready to agree as long as she could find her place in his arms. Indecision wrenched at her. If only, she thought, there could be a blinding revelation to help her.

But there would be no revelation. She and she alone could make this choice. Damiano had reminded her that she was a businesswoman with a clear-eyed view of life. But suddenly her view was blurred and she was torn in many directions. How could she choose?

The path stretched ahead of her, winding and twisting, promising, threatening, warning, tempting. And always at the end of it stood Damiano, his arms reaching for her.

'Say yes,' he told her.

'I—I don't know—'

'Say you'll marry me. Say it, Sally. You know that you must.'

'I—I don't—I can't—'

'Sally, *Sally.*'

The urgent cry from upstairs made them look up to see Pietro at the top of the stairs.

'It's your cell phone,' he called. 'I can hear it ringing in your room.'

'Thank you, I'm coming.'

'Let it ring,' Damiano said.

'No, I have to answer it.'

She didn't have to, but suddenly she needed to escape him with his power to fill her with confusion. She ran up the stairs and into her bedroom where her cell phone was shrilling. She answered and heard a male voice.

'Sally, it's me, Jim.'

Jim was the friend who'd alerted her to the job she'd applied for back in England. At any other time she would have been thrilled to hear from him.

'Jim, I'm sorry but just now—'

'Just listen, it's urgent. I've got good news. The job's practically yours. I overheard the boss talking, and you're the top candidate. I don't know why you had to take off just now, but you should get yourself back here fast.'

'I can't '

'You've got to. This is your big chance. Get on the first plane out of there.'

She drew a long, shaking breath, turning her head to look at Damiano, who was standing in the door, watching her.

'I can't,' she repeated.

'For pity's sake, why not?'

'Because—because—I'm thinking of getting married.' The words seemed to emerge of their own accord, drawn out of her by the intensity of Damiano's expression as he looked at her.

'Jim? Are you still there?'

'Yes, trying to believe what I've just heard. You? Married?'

'Does it sound so incredible that I should marry?'

'It does when you've got a great future here. This is one of the most important firms in London and they really want you. You could end up a partner. It's the big break you've always wanted.'

'Yes,' she said slowly.

'Sally, this is the chance of a lifetime, and if you pass it up it will never come again.'

Chance of a lifetime, said the voice in her head. *Never come again.*

'Sally, do you understand? This is it. The big moment. Seize it, or you'll regret it for ever.'

'For ever,' she murmured.

Damiano was still watching her. Their eyes met. The silence seemed to sing about her, echoing throughout the world.

'Sally, are you still there?' Jim's voice was sharp.

'Yes, I'm still here. And I—I have to tell you—that I'm staying here. Goodbye.'

As she set down the phone Damiano laid his hands on her shoulders.

'I wasn't expecting that,' he said.

'Neither was I. It just suddenly seemed—inevitable. I don't know why.'

She had been taken over by another self, with a will that was stronger than hers. And there was no way she could fight this other creature, because she knew in her heart that it was herself; another aspect of her inner nature, yet still herself. It wore a different mask, but the eyes that gazed on a world grown suddenly confusing were her own.

'I don't know why,' she repeated softly.

'I do. Because it *is* inevitable. Don't pretend not to understand. We were in tune with each other from the moment we met. You fitted in, with Pietro, with me, with everything. Can you deny it?'

'No,' she said slowly. 'I can't deny it. That first evening—it was as though we could read each other's mind.'

'And we could.'

'About some things, not everything.'

'Well, you know I'm a conniving character. But you'll always manage to get one step ahead. I'm more afraid of you than you ever will be of me.'

She stepped back and regarded him with her head on one side. 'That sounds like a pretty good basis for marriage. I reckon I can take the risk.'

'Good. And I do have one virtue. I'm a man of my word. You'll gain from this marriage, I promise.'

'I believe you.'

He leaned towards her and she braced herself

for the passionate kiss that was inevitable now. But his lips brushed her cheek for only a moment before he stepped back.

'We have a long road to travel,' he said quietly. 'And we need to take our time. There are things that can wait until you are ready.'

She understood his meaning. There would be no passion between them until she was safely in his possession. And perhaps he was right, she thought. His touch could excite her more than she wanted to admit, but she would be cautious and keep that to herself. He had predicted that she could get one step ahead of him, and he was more right than he knew. She made a mental note to keep things that way. At least for now.

FREE Merchandise is 'in the Cards' for you!

Dear Reader,

We're giving away FREE MERCHANDISE!

Seriously, we'd like to reward you for reading this novel by giving you **FREE MERCHANDISE** worth over $20. And no purchase is necessary!

You see the Jack of Hearts sticker above? Paste that sticker in the box on the Free Merchandise Voucher inside. Return the Voucher promptly...and we'll send you valuable Free Merchandise!

Thanks again for reading one of our novels—and enjoy your Free Merchandise with our compliments!

Pam Powers

Pam Powers

P.S. Look inside to see what Free Merchandise is **"in the cards"** for you!

We'd like to send you two free books like the one you are enjoying now. Your two books have a combined price of over $10, but they are yours to keep absolutely FREE! We'll even send you 2 wonderful surprise gifts. You can't lose!

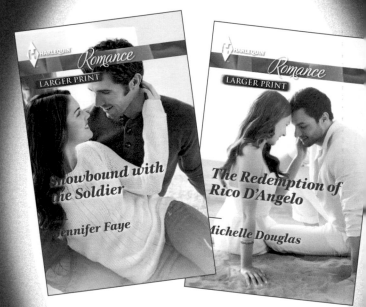

REMEMBER: Your Free Merchandise, consisting of **2 Free Books** and **2 Free Gifts**, is worth over $20.00! No purchase is necessary, so please send for your Free Merchandise today.

Get TWO FREE GIFTS!

We'll also send you two wonderful FREE GIFTS (worth about $10), in addition to your 2 Free books!

CHAPTER SEVEN

As LONG AS she lived she would remember the sight of Pietro's face when Damiano said, 'How would you like it if Sally stayed with us for ever?'

For the moment the boy's expression was blank. 'For ever?' he echoed, as though trying to understand what the word meant. 'For ever?'

Of course he doubted, she thought. He dreaded to be abandoned again.

'For ever?' he repeated.

Damiano nodded in her direction. 'Ask her.'

She dropped to one knee so that she could look Pietro in the eye.

'I'm staying,' she said, 'for as long as you want me.'

'But that's for ever and ever and ever and ever and ever.'

'Then that's how long I'm staying.'

He gazed in disbelief. 'Really?'

'Really.'

'Really?'

'Really.'

'Really?'

'Really.'

'And—you'll be—my mother?'

'If that's what you want.'

'We're getting married,' Damiano said.

Pietro's shriek of delight hit the ceiling and the next moment he'd flung his arms around Sally's neck, squeezing her so tightly that she gasped. She hugged him back, filled with pleasure at his welcome.

Then her joy was doubled when Damiano dropped to one knee, wrapping his arms about them both. For a moment the three of them stayed like that, locked together like the family they wanted to be. From his expression Sally knew that she'd given him exactly what he wanted. As if to confirm it he mouthed, 'Thank you.'

'When's the wedding?' Pietro demanded as the three of them eased apart. 'Tomorrow?'

'I'm afraid not,' Damiano said.

'Oh, please, let's have it tomorrow.'

'We have to get through some formalities first. Sally's English and we must get paperwork from England. But don't worry. She's ours now, and we won't let her go.'

Pietro nodded. 'Ours,' he said. 'All ours.'

'All yours,' Sally said fondly. 'And Toby's, of course.'

'Yes, yes, yes, I'll go and tell him. Toby—*Toby!*'

When Pietro had scampered away she said, 'It's lovely to see him so glad. But what do I have to do about papers?'

'You need to produce your English birth certificate, and a document stating that you're free to marry. They'll be taken to the nearest Italian Embassy to be translated and sent to us.'

'So much to do? Goodness, I must go back to England at once, and see to all this.'

'That won't be necessary,' Damiano said. 'I have a lawyer in London who can take care of everything.'

'But—'

'I said no. There's a lot for you to do here.'

She groaned. 'I see what it is. You think I won't come back. Do you trust me so little?'

'I trust you completely. I know you mean to come back, but something might happen while you're over there to make you stay. Look.' He pointed out of the window to where Pietro was in the garden, talking excitedly to Toby.

'I've never seen him so happy,' he said. 'I'll do what I must to keep him that way. If you return to England he'll be afraid, even if I tell him you're coming back. I won't put him through that.' He gazed at her intensely. 'Would you?'

'No,' she sighed. 'I hadn't thought of it that way.'

'Give me the details and I'll contact England now.'

After that things moved fast. He emailed his English lawyer, who called back that night to say the paperwork was in hand and he would bring it personally.

'Then we'll go to the local Civil State Office, and ask them to publish the banns,' Damiano told her. 'After another few days we'll be free to marry.'

'All this delay and formality just because I'm English,' she mused.

'But of course,' Damiano said. 'You're a deeply suspicious character. I've always known that.'

'Then I'm surprised you bother with me.'

'Ah, well, that's my problem. I have a weakness for suspicious characters.'

'Me too. So much more interesting than the other sort.'

They laughed together, and she knew a feeling of warmth and pleasure. The future looked hopeful.

In two days the lawyer arrived from London with the paperwork and the formalities were completed. A date for the ceremony was settled, two days before the end of Carnival. It would take place in the wedding suite of the Palazzo Leonese.

'You'll need some new clothes,' Damiano observed. 'The hotel dress shop will take care of all your needs. Don't worry about the bill.'

She found Helena, the manageress, ready with a supply of elegant clothes, one of which was clearly a wedding dress of pale cream satin. The sight of herself wearing it took her breath away.

So Cinderella can go to the ball, she thought. But what happens when midnight strikes?

She remembered how Damiano had annulled his marriage. Clearly Imelda had brought it on herself, but Mario's words, 'It was like he wiped her out of existence,' rang ominously.

Fulfil Damiano's desires and he would treat you with a warmth and charm that could overwhelm you. Offend him and you would cease to exist.

But then she looked back into the mirror at the new self she was becoming, a self she had never dared hope that she could be, and everything else was forgotten.

'Beautiful,' Helena said. 'Now you need another gown for the celebratory ball.'

She tried on three, walking back and forth before the mirrors. One had an innocent but fashionable simplicity. One was plainly cut, suggesting a woman of severe intelligence. Another was flamboyant, low in the bosom, daring, completely unlike the way she usually saw herself.

'I'll take this one,' she said.

'Good for you,' said a voice behind her.

She turned and saw Charlie.

'Thought I'd come and see how you were doing,' he said. 'Do they do men's clothes here as well?'

'Certainly,' said Helena. 'If you will come this way.'

It was no surprise when Charlie made a large choice. He looked handsome in everything, especially the suit he would wear to give her away.

'How much is it?' she murmured to him.

'I didn't ask. Damiano's paying.'

'Of course,' she sighed. 'Why didn't I think of that?'

'I can't imagine,' he said with an impish grin. 'You've had a fantastic piece of luck, so make the most of it.'

Fantastic piece of luck, she thought. Is that what it is? If all I cared about was money I suppose it would be luck, but—but—oh, I wish I knew what to think.

When they had finished Helena showed them the bill, the size of which almost made Sally dizzy. But she signed it. Even her own actions didn't seem in her control these days.

'Everything will be delivered tomorrow morning,' Helena announced.

'Can't I take anything with me now?' Sally asked. 'The house is just next door and Damiano might want to see them.'

'No, make him wait,' Charlie said. 'When a

man's that crazy about you it's best to play hard to get.'

Crazy about you. The words sang ironically in her ears.

It was what the world would think, but Damiano wasn't crazy about her.

Well, I'm not crazy about him, she thought defiantly. So that makes everything all right.

Damiano was out when they went home. He arrived an hour later. She hurried to meet him so that they could talk without Charlie.

'Did it go well?' he asked. 'Did you find what you wanted?'

'Yes, thank you. Here's the bill. It's much larger than I wanted it to be. I didn't know that Charlie—'

'I told him to go and get something for himself. We don't want him at our wedding looking like a down and out.'

'I suppose so, but look at the amount. He said you were paying.'

'Naturally, but in a couple of days you'll have all you need in your own bank account.'

'I don't have one here.'

'You do now. Here.'

He handed her a bunch of papers, which she examined, first with a smile, then with a gasp of horror.

Damiano had not only opened an account, he'd deposited a large amount of money.

'What's the matter,' he asked, seeing her dismay. 'Isn't it enough?'

'Enough? It's far too much. I never asked you for money.'

'That's irrelevant. A man naturally makes his wife an allowance.'

'I have money of my own, which I shall be bringing from England.'

'Good. But I consider myself indebted to you, and I pay my debts.'

'Which you will do by protecting Charlie. I don't want your money. I shall transfer it back to you.'

'And I shall tell the bank not to move it,' he said, sounding exasperated.

'Thus making a fool of me.'

'Not nearly as big a fool as you'd make of me if you refuse to take anything from me. That lump sum is my wedding gift. After that I shall make a monthly payment. Don't you realise that if you refuse it the gossip will be all around Venice in no time? How will that make me look?'

'Does your reputation depend on giving money to me?'

'It depends on my behaviour, my strength, my dignity. All of which you seem determined to smear with mud.'

'And what about my reputation?'

'I'm behaving with the propriety a groom is expected to show his bride. You haven't forgotten that you will be my bride, have you?'

'Well—in a way I will—'

'In every way. We will meet in the chapel and solemnly swear devotion to each other for the rest of our lives.'

From any other man this could be a declaration of love. But love had nothing to do with it, she knew.

Her head was spinning with ideas she didn't understand, something that happened very often in Damiano's company.

'Why does this make you angry?' he asked. 'From any other man you'd call it generosity, but from me it makes you suspicious. Why? Did you think I'd try to imprison you by keeping you poor?'

'No, but—well, I didn't think you'd make it so easy for me to cheat you. With an amount like that I could make a run for it.'

'But you won't. Keeping you poor would have been fatal. You'd have been brooding about escape all the time.'

Instead, the knowledge that she could afford to leave whenever she liked would keep her here. He had understood her perfectly.

'I told you,' he said. 'I make a fair bargain and

I keep it. I respect you enough to believe that you'll do the same.'

'Of c-course—thank you,' she stammered.

His words had touched a nerve. By behaving generously he'd made her as much his prisoner as if he'd locked the door. Just another instance of his shrewd and controlling nature.

He still looked doubtful but was too wise to pursue it.

He left her to go to his office, almost as though wanting to escape her. She found that Charlie had gone out again, so she went to her own room and sat studying the papers from the bank. Not for the first time she wondered what she was getting herself into. She was behaving differently, quite unlike herself.

At least, my usual self, she thought. I wonder where the other one is taking me.

After a while Charlie's face appeared around the door.

'Hello,' she said. 'What have you been up to?'

He came in. 'Mario's been showing me around. He's a great guy, knows all the places.'

'All the naughty places, you mean?'

'One or two. But he wouldn't take me inside in case it annoyed his brother. I told him Damiano would never know. But he says Damiano knows everything. One of those dubious places actually belongs to him.'

'But Mario still wouldn't take you in?'

'That's right. Said Damiano would hit the roof. Boy is that man a control freak! You'd better watch out when you're married to him. It'll be "Come here, go there. Do this, do that." He'll keep you short of money so that…'

His voice trailed off as he saw the papers on the table. 'What's this?'

'He's arranged a bank account for me.'

'And he's giving you this much? Oh, brother, you've really got him under your spell, haven't you?'

'Don't talk nonsense,' she said angrily. 'He's not in love with me any more than I am with him. It's for Pietro's sake, and this is his way of being fair to me.'

'Fair? Look, Sal, you don't have to stay here. You could take this money and run. Or is he tying it up so that you can't?'

'No,' she said. 'He's left me with complete freedom. He's an honourable man who deals fairly. He knows I won't take the money and run.'

'So you'll stay here and get some more out of him. I'll bet there's plenty still to come.'

'Get out,' she snapped, furious at his vulgar twist on the situation. 'I'm sick of you twisting everything to put Damiano in a bad light, so that you can justify your own selfishness.'

Charlie went to the door but before leaving he looked back at her with an ironic smirk.

'He's really got you just where he wants you, hasn't he?'

Reading terrible retribution in her face, he left quickly before she could throw something at him. His determination to think only the worst of Damiano roused in her a protective instinct that she hadn't known she had.

Why does he do it? she raged silently. Damiano's better than that. And he's worth far, far more.

He brought it on himself, she realised, by hiding his warmer feelings from the world. But not from her. With others his severe mask was kept in place virtually all the time. With her he sometimes let it slip, even if only briefly, suggesting the possibility of other masks, gentler, more attractive; masks that he might wear for a while before taking shelter again. Or that he might cast aside to reveal something deeper, even more intriguing.

That might happen with herself. Or it might never happen.

'I wonder,' she whispered. 'I wonder.'

Damiano had another surprise for her. For three hours he vanished with Mario and Charlie, returning later to reveal that they had spent the time in the hotel.

'The Leonese manager is leaving,' he said as they shared a drink by the canal. 'I've asked Mario to take over for a while. He's run places for me before and he has a talent for it. We've been around today, with Charlie. I think Charlie might well find a place there. He met the staff and I must admit that he charmed them. He could well have a future in hotel management.'

'You really think—?'

'Of course, he'll have to start at the bottom and learn to speak Italian. But I'll pay him a decent wage and he'll live with us. And as long as he's there Mario will take him under his wing. They get on well.'

'Yes,' Sally murmured. 'Mario's practically his hero. He's been taking him around Venice—'

'Going to all the places he shouldn't.' Damiano grinned. 'Mario's just what he needs. He's got his "adventurous" side—'

'Which is the bit Charlie likes,' Sally mused.

'Right. But actually he's got a "guardian angel" side too. So Charlie will be safe with him.'

'But how does Mario feel about being a guardian angel? Wouldn't he rather be out living the high life?'

'The high life has been a bit costly recently, and I've solved a few problems for him. Now I've asked a favour in return, and he's agreed, probably hoping that I'll help him out of the next mess.'

So he was pulling strings again, she thought. But she couldn't bring herself to blame him. He'd promised to protect Charlie and he'd found a way to do it that was better than anything she could have imagined. She could only respond by keeping her own side of the deal, and doing all she could for Pietro. And that too was what he'd intended to happen.

He's controlling me, she thought. But how can I complain when he's giving me so much that I want, and it feels so good?

She read his eyes and knew that he'd understood her thoughts and was waiting for her to reach a conclusion.

And there was only one possible conclusion.

'Thank you,' she said. 'This will be perfect for Charlie. Mario can talk sense to him in a way that I can't.'

'They're coming,' Damiano said, hearing voices in the corridor. 'Don't let them find us talking about them. They might be suspicious.'

'You mean they might suspect we were organising their lives?' she asked with a dramatic assumption of shock. 'How could they possibly think that?'

'Some people always believe the worst,' he said with a grin. 'Especially of me. Let's go.'

She had a brief glimpse of Mario and Charlie talking. Charlie seemed absorbed in Mario's words, and content in a way that was rare with him. The sight eased her heart.

Mario's revelations about his brother had inspired her to go online again to study him in greater detail than before. She discovered a powerful man with properties not only in Venice, but Rome and Milan, plus business interests that extended into other areas, and powerful friends in the political world, many of whom chose to stay at the Leonese when they were in Venice.

Now the word was out that he intended to take a wife, and everyone who knew him was curious. Nobody had ever expected this, and the news that the Leonese would celebrate Carnival with a costume party brought a flood of people anxious to join.

'*They're* coming?' Mario enquired, studying the list of attendees. 'All of them?'

'So they tell me,' Damiano conceded.

'You could have doubled the price of the tickets. I guess everyone wants to see Sally.'

'But they won't see me,' she said. 'Not really. I've got a costume and mask that will leave them wondering what I'm hiding.'

She had chosen a dress of deep gold satin, elegantly decorated with embroidery. Her mask was white with glistening gold decorations about the eyes. It covered her face almost completely, with just a little space left for her mouth. Gold feathers swirled around her head.

'That's a brilliant choice,' Mario told her when they all met up just before the ball. 'It'll keep them guessing.'

'Which means she's a true Venetian,' Damiano said, regarding her admiringly.

His own costume was in the eighteenth-century style, an elegant suit of black velvet, with a long coat and knee breeches. His mask was flesh-coloured and covered only the top half of his face, so that at first it wasn't clear that he was wearing a mask at all.

If you just looked quickly, Sally thought, you might think you were seeing his real face. You'd have to get closer to realise that it's partly hidden. Just like Damiano himself. I still don't know very much about him; what's real and what's concealed. Will he ever show me his true face?

But then, will I ever show him mine? Will I ever want to?

Mario began parading before them in a costume of jerkin and trousers, patterned with squares of red, green, blue and yellow.

'I'm Arlecchino,' he declared, bowing elaborately to Sally. 'Part servant, part clown.'

'Part idiot,' Damiano declared, grinning. 'You want to watch out for him, Sally. Arlecchino was a character in a lot of plays over the years, always getting up to mischief, then vanishing. No prizes for guessing why my brother likes to be him.'

'Not just your brother.' Sally chuckled. 'Mine too. Charlie bought a costume very like that. Mario told him it was the best way to be wicked and get away with it.'

'I deny that,' Mario said at once. 'You imagined it.' His manner became theatrical. 'Damiano, this lady is delusional. Never believe a word she says.'

'See what I mean?' Damiano said. 'Wicked.'

'I do my best,' Mario agreed, glad to see that Sally was enjoying the joke. 'How about this?' He put on his mask, which was black leather, leaving only his mouth free. A sharp horn rose from the crown.

'What's that?' she asked, pointing at it.

'It's a horn of the devil,' Mario said cheerfully. 'Only one, because I'm only half a devil.'

'Half's probably enough,' she agreed.

'But a second horn could be useful,' Charlie observed. 'I think I'll put a second one on my mask.'

'You're quite enough of a devil without help,' she informed him with sisterly candour.

Turning back to Mario, she indicated his uncovered mouth.

'Wouldn't you be safer from discovery if your mouth was hidden too?'

For answer he blew her a kiss. 'But then my pleasures would be restricted,' he said significantly.

'Ah, yes, I see,' she said. 'You couldn't put up with that.'

Damiano was glancing out of the window to where he could see guests arriving.

'Just about everyone is here,' he said. 'Time we joined them.'

CHAPTER EIGHT

TOGETHER THEY MADE their way through the connecting door into the hotel, and from there into the ballroom, where they were met by cheers.

Knowing what was expected of him, Damiano played his part to perfection, leading Sally onto the floor, then drawing her into his arms for a waltz. The music filled the air, seeming to flow through her, making her part of itself. She no longer had a will of her own. Life meant dancing through a distant universe with this mysterious man who smiled at her from behind his mask.

'Why are you looking so tense and nervous?' he murmured. 'People will think I'm forcing you to marry me.'

'You couldn't do that, not in this day and age.'

'But I have a reputation as a manipulating bully. You've accused me of it yourself.'

'Manipulator yes, bully no. You're far too clever for clumsy bullying.'

That made him laugh. She joined in, and everyone dancing near them nodded in satisfaction to see a couple so truly happy together.

He was a fine dancer, holding her firmly but gently, and she found herself moving with a skill that matched his. It was disappointing when courtesy demanded that they each attend to other people. In the arms of another partner she found herself thinking only of him, how strong and warm his body felt against hers.

After a while she saw Arlecchino bouncing across the floor to her.

'Shall we dance?' he asked, with an elaborate bow.

'Do I dare dance with the devil?' she teased.

'Tonight I am merely your servant.'

'I think I prefer a clown.'

His answer was an elaborate leap into the air, finishing with another bow. 'Then a clown you shall have.'

Laughing, she let him lead her onto the floor.

Like his brother, Mario was a fine dancer, lithe and energetic, holding her close in the waltz.

'I don't think you should hold me so tight,' she gasped after a while.

'I'm merely showing my respects to my sister-in-law,' he said theatrically. 'Do you accuse me of impropriety?'

'No, of course not.' But as she spoke she saw something in his eyes that gave her pause. There was an intensity of admiration there that she hadn't expected, and that was more than merely amusing.

'I think you should let me go,' she said.

'Yes, perhaps you're right,' he said with a regretful sigh.

As he led her from the floor he said, 'I'm sorry, Sally, I didn't mean to—you know. It's just that I think my brother's the luckiest fellow on earth. I know I shouldn't say that but—don't be mad at me.'

'I'm not,' she said truthfully.

She was too unused to male admiration to be offended by it. And it passed across her mind that it was a look she never saw in Damiano's eyes. Or expected to.

The evening was moving to its climax. Damiano signalled for silence and attention.

'I thank you all for coming here tonight, to honour my bride,' he said. 'I am a lucky man, as you can see, and I thank her for being ready to put up with me.'

He raised his glass in salute to her, as did everyone else in the room. Then there was more dancing. Many of the guests were business acquaintances, anxious to display their respect for the bride of a powerful man.

'How are you managing?' Damiano asked her after a while.

'Wonderfully. Everyone's nice to me, but it's a little hot in here. I need to go outside for a moment.'

Briefly she hoped that he would come with her, but someone called his name, so she headed for the garden alone.

She was vaguely aware of curious glances, some from people fascinated to know that this was Damiano's bride, the woman with the magic to conquer Venice's most stony-hearted man. The others came from the few folk who hadn't recognised her, and wondered who the masked figure might be.

A good question, she thought. I'm beginning to wonder myself.

It was peaceful in the garden. Pleasant as it was to be the centre of attention, she knew it was based on an illusion. Now she knew a mysterious desire to be alone, free from the need to pretend.

She was about to return to the ballroom when she heard two voices a few feet away, speaking in English.

'I must admit I'm a bit surprised to see Damiano taking a new wife at this precise moment,' said a woman.

Sally tensed, unable to move as a man replied, 'You mean at Carnival? But it's all so cheerful. Surely that's a good time to get married?'

'Carnival has special memories for Damiano.

That's when he finally won Gina after he'd given up hope. I was there at the party when she walked in, and I saw his face when he realised she'd come back to him. At first he simply couldn't believe he was seeing her, but as he walked across the floor to her his face lit up and his arms opened.'

'Really? It's not like Damiano to be demonstrative.'

'True,' the woman agreed. 'You never saw a man so happy. She threw herself into his arms and the two of them fled. We didn't see them again that night. Next thing we heard they were getting married.'

'And then she died.'

'Yes, their happiness was so short-lived. It makes you wonder how he's feeling now. Can he bear to play the lover of another woman when he must be haunted by those memories tonight?'

'Aren't you being a bit sentimental?' the man asked ironically.

'Probably. I expect he's madly in love with this new bride and has forgotten all about Gina.'

Sally hurried away. She didn't want to be discovered now, while she was so shaken by what she had heard.

Madly in love with his new bride. Nothing could be further from the truth. If anything his marriage was another affirmation of his love for

Gina. For the sake of their son he would do anything, even marry a woman he didn't love.

How well he'd played his part, she thought, honouring her, showing her off with apparent pride, concealing his true feelings.

Whatever they were.

He was waiting for her at the entrance to the ballroom.

'There you are. I was worried about you.'

'I'm sorry, I shouldn't have left you alone.'

He took her hand.

'Perhaps it was all getting a little much for you,' he said gently. 'You look tired. Why don't you slip quietly away and leave me to bid everyone farewell?'

He was right, she thought. She needed to be alone, to think about what she'd heard, and reinforce her defences. And somewhere in her heart she knew that he was glad to bring the evening to an end. He'd behaved perfectly, but now the strain was catching up with him. He needed to be away from the crowd congratulating him on his bride. And he needed to be away from the bride herself. That was the truth.

She said her goodbyes and departed. Once back in her room she stripped off the extravagant costume and mask, and regarded herself in the mirror.

'The is me,' she said. 'The real me. The only

me.' But then she sighed, regarding her lean figure and blank face. 'Oh, dear. Not very impressive.'

She thought of the evening behind her when she had been officially the star, while secretly knowing that she was playing second fiddle.

The stand-in, she thought with a sigh. The understudy, performing because the one he really wanted wasn't available any more.

But then her sensible side reappeared and she sighed again; this time with exasperation with herself.

Oh, stop being difficult, Sally. You agreed to this as a deal, with something gained on both sides. He's keeping his side so shut up and stop complaining.

From her window she saw the crowd stream away from the hotel and the lights go out.

At last she heard Damiano come upstairs and go to his room. She waited, tense and hopeful, and to her relief there was a knock on her door. She opened it to find him there, stripped of his dramatic costume, now in pyjamas and dressing gown. He was holding two glasses of wine, one of which he held out to her. She took it and ushered him in.

'I'm sorry to have run away.'

'It's all right,' he said, sitting on the bed. 'You were marvellous. Everyone admired you.'

She didn't believe it. He was being polite, saying the things a bridegroom was expected to say. But his eyes suddenly closed, like a man surrendering to forces too strong for him, and her heart was touched.

'It's a sad time for you, isn't it?' she asked gently.

He opened his eyes. 'Why do you say that?'

'I know you're trying to look cheerful because of our wedding, for my sake. But it's really a shame that all this is happening just now, during Carnival.' She paused, unsure whether to pressure him further. But the need to know more about him was overwhelming.

'I know that Carnival has a special meaning to you because of Gina,' she said quietly.

'How do you know that?'

'I heard someone talking about her tonight, how she was away for a while. But she came back during one of the parties. You saw her across the room and she threw herself into your arms.'

He uttered a soft groan and dropped his head, as though the memory was unendurable. For a moment she nearly backed off, yet the hope of being in his confidence tempted her to urge him further.

'You must have had a wonderful reunion,' she ventured.

'Yes, we did. I could hardly believe it then

and I can still hardly believe it, even now—' He stopped, suddenly self-conscious. 'I'm sorry. What am I thinking of to be talking of her just before I marry you? Please forgive my appalling manners.'

'There's nothing to forgive,' she insisted. 'You're talking because I'm encouraging you. Damiano, we're not in love. We both understand that. We're marrying because we each gain something we want, and we like each other enough to make it work. We can be good friends. Can you talk about her to anyone else?'

He shook his head.

'Then talk to me. Let me be your best friend, the person you trust and confide in. It won't be the same as you enjoyed with her, but it might just give you a kind of contentment.'

He regarded her as if wondering if he'd heard properly, and how he should understand what she was saying.

'Do you really mean that?' he asked at last.

'Yes, I really mean it. And I always will.'

'Thank you,' he whispered. He took her hands between his and lowered his head to kiss them. 'Thank you.'

She tightened her hands on his to cope with the tension surging through her.

'Now we know we can talk freely,' she said. 'So tell me everything about how things happened between you and Gina. She was English, wasn't she? How did you meet?'

'Her brother had a shop on one of the islands. I went there one day and fell in love with her in the first moment. I wanted to marry her, but she had ambitions to be a model, and she went back to England fairly soon because she'd been offered an assignment.

'She had a fairly good career, not as successful as she hoped, but good enough to keep her trying. If she had a few weeks off she'd come out here and we could be together, but it seemed a very one-sided relationship. I adored her and she knew it, but she kept a certain emotional distance. She was charming to me, but she didn't return my passion and my embraces had to be restrained. When we met it was always because I'd gone to see her. She didn't come to me. This went on for several years.'

'Years?'

'Yes. I often told myself that enough was enough, that I should break it off and return to having a life of my own, one that she didn't dominate. But I could never kill the hope. She was worth waiting for, and I was sure that one day my love would come to mean so much to her that she would have to return it. But then she went away again, for much longer this time, and I thought I'd lost her for ever.

'But on the night of the ball a miracle happened. I saw a lovely mask, and I knew at once that she was the person behind it. She hadn't even told me she was coming, just appeared out of the blue, like a magical apparition.

'That night she became mine. As we lay together I knew that dreams can come true. She gave herself to me with all the love in her nature.

'After that we belonged to each other, heart and soul. I begged her to marry me and we set the wedding for the soonest possible date. The time that followed was the happiest I'd ever known. When we learned that she was pregnant I couldn't believe that heaven could be so kind. The future seemed to stretch before us, an endless road full of infinite joy. And then—'

His voice choked off suddenly and his head drooped. Now she couldn't see his face but she didn't need to. She knew it was transformed with grief in a way she didn't want to see. She'd spoken bravely about being his friend, defining their relationship in a way that they could both endure.

For the moment.

In time their closeness might develop another dimension, but just now she must live in hope.

Damiano raised his head again and she saw the glisten of tears on his face.

'And then she died,' he murmured. 'And it was my fault.'

'No, it wasn't. Don't say that.'

'I gave her the child whose birth killed her. But for that she'd still be alive today. It haunts me and it always will. She opened her arms to me because she wanted the life I could give her, but I destroyed her.'

She struggled for words that might comfort him, but there were no words. Deep inside he carried a burden of guilt that, however unjustified, tormented him night and day. Her heart ached for his pain and her own helplessness.

'Part of me died with her,' he went on. 'I would have died completely but for the child she left me. Pietro is her son and mine.'

'Yes,' she murmured. 'In him you are united for ever with her. And while you have him you'll never completely lose her.'

'Thank you,' he whispered. 'Thank you, dear Sally.' He laid his lips against her hand.

'I'm here for you,' she whispered. 'And I always will be.'

'Always,' he echoed. 'There was a time when that word tormented me, when I couldn't believe that anything could be for always. But you give me faith again.'

She laid her lips gently against his. For a tense moment she waited for his response, wondering if he would take her in his arms and turn his affectionate words into actions. But he drew back.

'Goodnight,' he whispered. 'Tomorrow we'll—we'll talk some more.'

He rose and went to the door.

'Goodnight,' he said again, and departed quickly.

She stayed motionless, trying to sort out her own thoughts and feelings. She had been briefly tempted to embrace him and take matters further, but every instinct told her this was not the time. Absorbed in his memories of Gina, the great love of his life, he was not ready to turn to her.

The time would come, she thought. And if she could be patient, it would be all the sweeter.

Now things moved fast. The date was set, the hotel's wedding chapel was booked. Mario was to be the best man. Charlie would give her away.

Damiano introduced her to Luisa, whose job it was to organise everything. She was an elderly woman with a friendly air and a strong sense of humour. She and Sally took to each other at once.

'Let me show you the chapel,' she said. 'It's as fine as anything you'll ever see.'

That was an understatement. Like the rest of the palazzo the chapel was several hundred years old, with a soaring roof, elaborate decorations and an air of luxury. Sally gazed up at the ceiling in wonder, trying to imagine herself against this glorious background. It was hard to believe, but so much was happening to her than she could ever have imagined.

'They all want to be married here,' Luisa told her. 'You wouldn't believe some of the famous people who've chosen this rather than anywhere else.'

She gave a brief list, enjoying Sally's look of startled disbelief.

'Him?' Sally exclaimed at one of the more glamorous names. 'Surely not. He's a big film star.'

'I'm not kidding you. Come and see the files.'

She took Sally through a door at the back of the chapel, and opened a large book full of wedding pictures. Sally browsed through them, noting the well-known names with interest and amusement.

But at the very end of the book she found something that made her grow still.

The picture showed a bride and groom standing close together, gazing into each other's eyes, so absorbed in each other that the rest of the world might not have existed.

Gina and Damiano.

She could just recognise Gina. It was the difference in Damiano that took her breath away. This young man was gentle, vulnerable, open to the world. His adoration of his bride was written all over his face. As long as she was his he cared nothing who knew how he felt.

She thought of the man he had become now, hard-faced, emotionally armoured, sadly different from the eager boy so clearly shown in the picture.

'Is anyone there?'

The sound of Damiano's voice made her shut the book quickly and hide it away. He must not find her looking at the picture of him with the wife he'd loved as he would never love herself.

'I'm here,' she called, returning to the chapel. 'Luisa has been showing me around. It's a magnificent place. You don't think perhaps it's a little too magnificent for me? We could tie the knot somewhere else.'

Subtly she was giving him the chance to escape marrying here where Gina's ghost lingered.

'No, it must be here,' he said. 'If we didn't use the hotel chapel eyebrows would be raised. Pietro would be worried in case our marriage wasn't real.'

And Pietro was the reason it was all happening, she remembered. How foolish of her to have forgotten that.

Luisa bustled in again.

'Let me show you your dressing room,' she said. 'It's right next door and it's where you'll get ready on the day.'

There were two rooms where she would be attended by a maid and a make-up artist, both provided by the hotel. Then she would be ready to step onto the 'stage' playing an unfamiliar role, wearing a mask she didn't completely understand.

Luisa took her to the hotel jeweller's shop, where the assistant measured Sally's finger, and handed over a ring. Then she produced another ring designed for a male hand. Luisa signed for both on Damiano's behalf, and took possession of them.

It was like being part of a well-oiled machine, Sally thought, feeling slightly dizzy.

Luisa came with her into Damiano's house.

'Here's the ring that you'll give him,' she said, pressing a small packet into her hand. 'I wish you every happiness.'

She walked away to his office, to hand over the other ring, Sally guessed. She could faintly hear the sound of their voices, and hurried away to her room.

Studying the ring, she found it plain and gold. She wondered about the one Gina must have given him, and guessed he kept it hidden away somewhere like a sacred relic.

After half an hour he knocked on her door.

'Did everything go well?' he asked.

'It all went as well as it possibly could.'

'Splendid. Then let me show you the sleeping arrangements.'

He led her to his room, which she would soon share with him.

'You can keep your present room as well,' he told her. 'It'll be somewhere to retreat when you find me impossible to endure.'

'Thank you,' she said with a faint smile. 'I dare say in time I'll learn to put up with you, but let's not rush it.'

'Very wise.'

She got the message. Damiano's room would be officially hers because that was what everyone would expect. The reality of their 'marriage' must remain private to themselves.

That might be hard, she thought, looking at the bed. It was wide, even for a double bed, but there was no barrier between the man and the woman who would share it. She wondered if this was where he'd slept with Gina.

I might need to slip away to my own room quite often, she mused. That's probably what he's hoping.

Downstairs they found Pietro waiting for them, looking worried.

'Is something wrong?' Sally asked.

'It's your honeymoon,' he said. 'You haven't arranged it yet. Look, I've got lots of brochures about places for you to go.'

It was the one thing they hadn't thought of. Now Damiano's expression told her that for once he'd been caught off-guard. Inspiration came to her.

'But we're not going away at all,' she said. 'We wouldn't enjoy it without you. And you can't come with us because you've got to go to school. So we're going to spend the honeymoon here, and in your spare time you can show me around Venice. I'm longing to see everything about this lovely place.'

Pietro gave a gasp of delight and looked eagerly at his father for confirmation. Damiano nodded at his son, then nodded again at Sally. There was no doubt that she'd done the right thing.

When Pietro had raced away to tell Toby the good news, she said, 'I suppose I shouldn't really have backed you into a corner without telling you first, but what else could I do?'

'Nothing. You did well and I'm in complete agreement.' He added wryly, 'But the next time you accuse me of ordering people about like puppets I shall remind you of this.'

'Yes, I suppose I did the same, but, after all, I'm learning from a master. And I dare say there are still plenty of tough tactics you can teach me.'

'Do you know, I'm beginning to wonder if there's anything I can teach you about conniving. But your idea is brilliant. I'm full of admiration. And that seems to be that. Everything is in place.'

'Everything,' she agreed, wondering what 'everything' really meant. 'I must go now. I've got some emails to send.'

'Me too. Goodbye until supper.'

CHAPTER NINE

THE NIGHT BEFORE the wedding Damiano said, 'There's an old wedding tradition in Venice. As she walks down the aisle the bride finds a child in her way. He needs help, so she gives him what help she can, and everyone knows she'll be a good mother. It dates back ages, but some brides still like to include it for sentimental reasons.'

'And you want me to include it for Pietro?'

Pietro wants you to include it. This afternoon he asked if I thought you'd do it. It would mean a lot to him.'

'Of course I will.'

'Let's go up and tell him.'

They found Pietro sitting up in bed.

'She said yes,' Damiano said. 'I told you she would.'

Pietro flung his arms around her, burying his face. She hugged him back, meeting Damiano's eyes and seeing in them his pleasure and satisfaction at his son's happiness.

'Goodnight, my son,' he said.

'Goodnight, Papa. Goodnight, Mamma.'

It was the first time he'd actually called her by that name and it brought tears to her eyes.

'Goodnight, my son,' she said huskily.

His beaming look was her answer, and they hugged each other blissfully for a minute.

'Sleep now,' she said.

'Yes, Mamma.' He snuggled down.

'He loves calling you that,' Damiano murmured as they left the room.

'I love it too. I wonder if any stepmother has ever been so warmly welcomed.'

'To him, you are more than just a stepmother. You're his mother now.'

'Yes, that's what I am.'

She thought he might have added that she would be a wife as well as a mother, but he said no more.

'Come with me a moment,' he said.

At his bedroom door he paused, went inside and emerged with a large box in his hand. 'I haven't yet given you a wedding present,' he said. 'Let's go to your room first.'

When they were there he opened the box to reveal a heavy diamond necklace.

'Oh, it's—it's beautiful,' she gasped. 'Put it on for me.'

He settled it around her neck while she gazed

into the mirror, trying to believe that this was really her, wearing the necklace of such dazzling glitter. She knew little of jewellery but clearly this was wickedly expensive.

'You didn't have to do this,' she breathed.

'But I did. This is my thank you for what you're doing. Sally, I think you hardly know what you've given me. When I see the happiness in my son's face I know a new happiness myself, a happiness I never thought to know again. And it's all due to you. Take this with my eternal gratitude.'

'But I-I don't have anything for you,' she stammered. 'I didn't know what to get you as a gift.'

'You've already given me the greatest gift I shall ever know.'

They surveyed their reflections, with him standing just behind her. Their eyes met in the mirror.

'Perfect,' he said. 'I'd like you to wear it tomorrow. Everyone who sees it will know how much you mean to me.'

He removed the necklace and replaced it in the box.

'Get a good night's sleep,' he said. 'Tomorrow will be a big day and—well—goodnight.'

He kissed her cheek and left the room. She followed him to the door and watched him go down the corridor without looking back. Then she went to her window and stood still, trying to get her thoughts in order.

A big day, Damiano had said. But it was more than a big day. It was the start of a new universe, one that she was plunging into with a recklessness that was normally alien to her.

She was leaving her country to live in a strange land, married to a man she'd known only a short time. Yet with every fibre of her being she was certain that she was doing the right thing—not because he was rich and showered her with valuable gifts. But because his need made him reach out to her in a way she couldn't resist.

Below her a gondola appeared, with two lovers locked in each other's arms, oblivious to the world around them.

She watched until they were out of sight. Then closed the window and went to bed.

Next morning they would not meet before the wedding. She breakfasted with Charlie, then slipped into the hotel and went to the rooms set aside for the bride's preparation. A maid helped her dress, then the make-up artist got to work. When she had finished she nodded in satisfaction at her own handiwork.

'A beautiful bride,' she said, and departed.

Alone, Sally had to admit that the woman looking back at her from the mirror was closer to being a beauty than she'd ever seen before.

But who is that? she thought. Me? Or just another mask?

There was a knock on the door. Expecting to find Mario, she opened it.

But outside there was a woman with a hard, determined face. For a moment Sally was bewildered. Then she remembered the two photographs she had seen by Pietro's bed, and she gasped as she realised who this was.

'I guess that means you know me,' the woman said with a wry smile that was almost a sneer.

She had aged since the photograph and now confronted the world aggressively. But there was no doubt this was Imelda.

'Yes, I know you,' Sally said, trying to speak through her shock. 'You were—Damiano's wife.'

The woman gave a bitter laugh. 'That's one way of putting it. Are you going to let me in, or are you afraid of me? Perhaps you ought to be.'

'I'm not afraid of you,' Sally said untruthfully.

She stood back and Imelda swept into the room, moving in a queenly manner that implied that everything was her right.

'His wife,' she repeated. 'It's how I thought of myself, as his wife. But I soon had to face the truth, that he saw me as a servant, hired for a purpose and married only to keep me tied to him.'

'You make him sound like a monster,' Sally protested. 'But he isn't. He cares for people—'

'Some people perhaps. He was crazy about Gina. He still is. And Pietro is all he has left of her, so he loves him for her sake. But the rest of us are just useful objects to be moved around as it suits him.'

Mounting temper made Sally say, 'Perhaps he isn't the only one. You abandoned that vulnerable child when it suited you.'

'I had to save myself before it was too late. Now I'm here to warn you before you make the same mistake I did. If you marry him you'll regret it for ever. He's using you as he used me. He wasn't in love with me and he's not in love with you.'

Sally faced her, meeting the other woman's bitter eyes with an expression that was cool and seemingly untroubled, although inside a storm was taking hold.

'That's fine,' she said, 'because I'm not in love with him. It's a fair and equal bargain.'

'Hah!' Imelda's crack of derisive laughter was like the wielding of a weapon. 'Fine talk. You think so now, but he'll lure you into loving him for his own convenience.'

'He won't be able to. You don't know me any more than he knows me. I'm perfectly safe.'

'You think you're safe,' Imelda sneered. 'But

nobody is safe from that man's determination to make the world dance to his tune. He does everything for his own ends.'

'But so do I,' Sally insisted. 'However bad you believe he is, I promise you I'm just as bad. Maybe worse, because I can think of schemes he'd never dream of.'

'So maybe you can make him sorry? That'll be something to look forward to.'

'Don't hope for too much,' said a voice behind them.

Damiano was standing in the doorway. Before their astonished eyes he walked into the room and addressed Sally, giving Imelda only the briefest glance.

'It's time we were going to the chapel,' he said. 'We thought you'd have joined us before now. Not changed your mind, have you?'

'Not at all,' she said in a determinedly cheerful voice. 'When I've made a decision I stick to it through thick and thin.'

He turned to Imelda. 'Sorry to disappoint you. Nice try. But it was never going to work. Sally and I understand each other too well for anyone to get between us.'

'You heard her say she doesn't love you,' Imelda sneered.

'Yes, and I heard her say we made a fair and

equal bargain. Love has nothing to do with it. Now I think you should go.'

She pulled a face at him, then turned to depart. But suddenly Pietro appeared. At once his face brightened and he began to run towards them.

'Mamma,' he squealed. 'Mamma!'

Both Sally and Damiano tensed, dreading what must surely happen now. Pietro had been heart-broken when his 'mother' had abandoned him, and now he would suffer more pain.

But Imelda might not have existed as he scampered past her to throw himself into Sally's arms.

'Everyone's waiting for you,' he said. 'Charlie said you must have got last-minute nerves and made a run for it.'

'No,' she said quickly. 'I would never run away from you.'

'What about Papa?'

'Well, I might run away from him, but not you. Never you.'

He giggled, glancing up to catch his father's reaction and was rewarded with a cheerful grin. For a moment father and son held each other's eyes, while Sally fell silent, enjoying the sight.

The only one not happy was Imelda, for whom the moment seemed to sum up her resentment.

'You think you're clever, don't you?' she muttered to Sally. 'But you'll find out what a mistake you've made. Just wait and see.'

She turned and marched away. Pietro watched her leave, seemingly untroubled.

'You handled her brilliantly,' Damiano said in a voice too low for Pietro to hear.

'You heard what we said?'

'Everything.'

So he'd heard her declare that she didn't love him and never would. For another couple that would have been disaster, but they were different. For them it could even be a source of strength.

'A fair and equal bargain,' he repeated. 'You said it perfectly. And now I think it's time for us to get married. That was the bargain, wasn't it?'

'Fair and square,' she said, extending her hand. He shook it.

'I'm sorry that happened,' Damiano said. 'You shouldn't have had to meet Imelda like that.'

'Don't worry. She didn't tell me anything I didn't already know.'

'You mean you already know that I'm the monster she called me?'

'I've always known that. But I'm a monster too. You'll make some shocking discoveries. Perhaps you should run from me before it's too late.'

He shook his head, taking her hand in his and speaking softly.

'It's already too late. Even without a wedding ceremony, I belong to you and you belong to me.' His grasp tightened. 'Don't think of escape. Ever.'

'I don't want to escape,' she promised. 'I want something completely different.'

'I just hope it includes me.'

'Who else could it possibly include?'

'That was the perfect thing to say.' He lowered his head to lay his lips tenderly on hers. She kissed him back, relishing the sweetness that went through her at his touch. He drew back a little and looked down on her with a smile.

'I'm going to make sure of you while I have the chance,' he said softly.

As if by a signal Mario and Charlie appeared in the door.

'Everyone's waiting,' Mario called. 'And you—' he addressed Pietro. 'Time to get into position with—you know what.'

Pietro darted out of the room.

'You know what?' Sally asked. 'What's that?'

'You'll find out,' Charlie said impishly.

'She certainly will,' Mario said, leading the way out. After a brief nod Damiano followed his brother.

'Come along, sister,' Charlie said. 'Time for me to give you away.'

The moment was here. If she had any doubts this was her last chance to say so. But she took his arm and together they headed for the chapel.

Now she could hear the music, and through the open doors she could see that the groom and best man had taken up their positions. The chapel was crowded with friends and business acquaintances.

'Ready?' Charlie asked.

Was she really ready? she wondered. But it was too late to ask that now.

'Yes,' she said firmly, taking his arm. 'I'm ready.'

They began to advance. There was Damiano with Mario by his side.

His eyes were fixed on her as though he was stunned by an approaching vision. But who did he see? she wondered. Herself or the ghost of Gina? And when he faced the truth, would she see disillusion in his eyes?

But before she reached him she saw something else.

'Pietro,' she murmured.

He was waiting for them just ahead, ready and eager to play his role. And he was not alone. Beside him was Toby, wagging his tail excitedly.

'They let you bring Toby in?' Sally whispered to the child.

'Not really,' Pietro said. 'I just sort of—slipped him in quietly.'

'What's that dog doing in here?' came a male voice.

A man in an usher's uniform was approaching.

'That animal can't stay here,' he said.

'But he's my friend,' Pietro protested.

'And my friend too,' Sally said. 'We're a family, all of us. How could I get married without my friends and family?'

The usher looked about to tear his hair out. The sight of the groom approaching unsettled him even more, but Damiano's manner was cheerful.

'Is everything all right?' he asked.

'There's no problem about Toby being here, is there?' she said. 'He's perfectly behaved.'

'But—' the usher began.

'These decisions are made by Signora Ferrone,' Damiano said with a significant glance at Sally, indicating that she had already acquired official status as his wife. 'If she is happy there is no problem.'

'And if Pietro and Toby are happy, I'm happy,' she said.

The usher retreated hastily. There were smiles from the crowd, and even a hint of applause from those who recognised that Sally had played her part perfectly. Now everyone knew that she would be a loving mother to the child who was hugging her so ecstatically.

But the greatest pleasure came from the look of warmth and gratitude Damiano gave her, and the way he mouthed, 'Well done.'

He returned to his place, now watching her with a smile. The procession resumed, Sally supported by Charlie, Pietro holding her other hand, Toby trotting obediently beside his young master.

For her sake the ceremony was held in English.
Sally had carefully studied papers given to her
by Luisa, and considered herself ready for everything. Even so, there was one question that made
her pause a little.

'Are you here willingly to make this marriage
of your own free choice?'

Your own free choice. She looked up at Damiano, wondering if he could truly declare that.

But his face revealed nothing as he asserted
his glad consent . A moment later she was able
to reply in the same controlled manner.

It was time for the exchange of rings, and now
Sally found another surprise awaiting her. She'd
known that Pietro was happy about this marriage,
but nothing could have prepared her for what happened next. When Mario, acting as best man,
produced the ring to give to his brother, he first
glanced at Pietro. The two nodded at each other.
Mario gave him the ring, and it was Pietro who
handed it to Damiano.

Nothing could have more clearly shown his
total acceptance of Sally into the family. Damiano
smiled at his son, then at Sally, as though wanting
to be sure that she understood. She smiled back
at Pietro, conveying her thanks.

But now Damiano's face grew serious again,
almost sad, as though a new thought had occurred
to him, one that obscured all others. He took her

hand in his, sliding the ring onto her finger and speaking the words that promised love and fidelity. In return she made the same vow, wishing his eyes would reveal something more, but they remained distant. She wondered if he was recalling the moment from his first wedding when he and Gina had bound themselves to each other, and he had rejoiced at the blissful prospect of life ahead.

It was time for the groom to kiss the bride. Putting his hands on either side of her face, he laid his lips on hers and stayed motionless for a moment. There was no pressure in his kiss, but the feel of it was sweet, filling her with sudden emotion.

He drew back, smiling.

'Now we are man and wife,' he said.

The choir burst into song as they turned to depart. Damiano drew her arm through his and led her back down the aisle with a broad smile on his face. To strangers it might seem the happy smile of a groom who'd secured the woman he loved. But to Sally it had more of the triumphant air of a man who'd achieved a great victory. Not for the first time Damiano Ferrone had got exactly what he wanted.

All the resources of the hotel were focused on making this the wedding of the year with the most fashionable food served to the most glamorous guests. There were gasps at the sight of the bride in her glittering diamond necklace, and some lively muttered conversations about the likely value of the jewels.

There were speeches. Damiano informed the crowd that he was the luckiest man in the world and everyone toasted the bride.

At last it was time for dancing. As the music started he led her onto the floor and drew her close for a waltz. As they turned gently in each other's arms the guests regarded them with admiration. Some of them even applauded the couple who looked the perfect picture of newly wedded bliss.

Everyone could see that Damiano was smiling with pleasure at his bride, and saying something to her with great fervour. Of course he was declaring his passion, they thought.

Sally did not expect a declaration of passion, but she read in his eyes a warmth that lifted her spirits.

'You were wonderful today,' he said. 'You did everything I wanted, better than I'd dared to hope.'

'I'm glad I didn't disappoint you. I was afraid of getting something wrong,' she admitted.

'You? You couldn't get anything wrong. Whatever you touch turns to gold.'

She laughed. 'Thank you, kind sir. The perfect speech, just what the groom is supposed to say to his bride.'

'No, I mean it. When Pietro turned up with Toby, any other woman would have made a mess of it, but you got it exactly right. Did you really not know in advance what he was going to do?'

'I knew he was going to be there because you'd told me, but I didn't know about Toby.'

'And when he insisted on being the one to hand me the ring to give you—that was his way of saying that we had his blessing.'

'Yes, it's nice to have that.'

'He's happier than I ever thought to see him again, and you've done that for him. Thank you with all my heart.'

She knew a faint twinge of disappointment that all his praise was for her achievements. A warm comment about her looks would have been pleasant. But she admonished herself for the thought. They had a deal and he was living up to his word, as he'd promised.

At last it was time for the guests to leave. Arms wrapped around each other, the bridal couple waved and smiled their farewells, then turned and climbed the stairs together, which was what everyone wanted to see.

Pietro had gone up ahead and was waiting for them in his room, with Toby.

'Are you my mamma now?' he asked.

'After the way you welcomed me today, of course I am. Yours and Toby's.'

She hugged him, conscious of Damiano's eyes on them, full of warmth. Deep inside she had a sweet feeling of triumph. This day had gone perfectly.

They bid the child goodnight and went slowly along the corridor to the room that was now theirs. Once inside he brushed her veil gently back from her face, then laid his hands on her shoulders.

She waited, trying to read his expression and guess his next words.

'You must be exhausted. Get to bed quickly, and sleep well.'

He saw the brief questioning glance she gave him, and said quickly, 'I'm grateful to you for everything you're doing. You were wonderful today. But I promised you that I wouldn't rush things, and I'll keep my word. When you're ready— well—'

He dropped his hands and stepped away towards the door.

'I'll be back soon,' he said before he left.

Thus allowing her time to undress in private, she realised. He couldn't have made it plainer that such desire as he might have for her was strictly controlled.

It was a sad moment. The happiness of the day

had almost made her forget the real reason for everything that was happening. But there would be no loving husband to undress her for their wedding night, and that was the reality. Common sense demanded that she remove her own clothes and hang them up neatly.

Common sense had never seemed so dreary. As she lay down in bed she wondered if Damiano intended to come back at all.

Returning half an hour later, Damiano found the room in darkness. Sally was lying on the far side of the bed, still and silent so that he couldn't be sure if she was awake.

He undressed and eased himself into the bed, moving gently so as not to disturb her. Drifting back over the day, his mind fixed on the moment when he'd heard her say, 'I'm not in love with him… I'm perfectly safe.'

Had she said it to shut Imelda up, or was it true that she didn't love him and was sure she never would?

Better if it was true, he thought. That would make their life together a lot simpler. Without love he could never hurt her. It was definitely the most satisfactory way.

He repeated that to himself several times.

There was a slight movement from her side of

the bed. He leaned towards her, reaching out his hand, laying it gently on her shoulder.

I'm not in love with him.

The words seemed to scream in his mind so forcefully that he looked around, fearful in case they were not alone. He removed his hand. To go further, after what he'd heard, would be foolish.

Lying motionless, Sally waited tensely for his next move. His hand on her shoulder had been gentle, the prelude to the soft caress that would start their wedding night. He would touch her again, drawing his fingers softly across her skin, tempting her to move towards him.

She drew a long breath, feeling her heartbeat grow stronger as she anticipated what must come next. She would turn to face him, moving closer, letting him know silently that she was ready to be his wife in every sense of the word. For much of today they had done what the world expected to see, but now they were alone and could do what their senses demanded.

Memories whirled through her: his mouth on hers as they kissed during the ceremony; the way he'd held her as they danced; the warmth in his eyes; the intensity in his voice as he'd said, 'You were wonderful today.'

She'd lied to Imelda, claiming that she was safe from him and always would be. The truth was that she would never be safe from this aching need to feel his touch, caress him in return, tempt him further. Now she knew why no other man had been able to arouse her desire. Deep inside she'd been waiting for this one man to caress her willing flesh and reveal to her the secrets of passion, so long concealed. If only he would stretch out his hand to her again.

But at last she realised that he wouldn't do that. He felt bound by his promise to keep a polite distance, at least for now. The next move must come from her. Slowly she eased herself around so that she was facing him.

'Are you all right?' he asked.

'Yes, I'm fine—'

'Then go to sleep. It's been a long, hard day for you. For me too. I haven't felt this worn out for ages. Get some rest, and tomorrow we can enjoy ourselves. Goodnight.' He patted her shoulder, and turned away, seeming to fall asleep at once.

'Goodnight,' she said forlornly.

Outside stars gleamed and the moon shone down on the brilliant city. In the darkness of the bedroom two people lay still and quiet, eyes open, staring into space, wondering what the future held.

CHAPTER TEN

IT WAS SALLY who awoke first, and lay listening to the quiet room. From behind her she could just hear the sound of steady breathing. Turning slowly, she saw Damiano lying with his back to her. She edged towards him carefully, anxious not to awaken him, leaning over his shoulder just far enough to make out his face on the pillow.

Suddenly he moved, twisting around towards her so suddenly that she had to back off quickly, unwilling to let him find her like this after the way he'd kept his distance on their wedding night. She just managed to get out of his reach as he settled facing her.

His eyes were still closed and now she discovered him as never before. At first she'd seen him in commanding mode. Later she'd witnessed his other selves, one businesslike but friendly, and another, humorous, pleasant, even sometimes gentle. But now he looked vulnerable, unprotected, as he'd been in the photograph of him with Gina on their wedding day. This was the first time the living man had appeared to her defenceless, and she knew a sudden temptation to touch his face, caressing it softly until he awoke and smiled at her.

But he wouldn't smile, she knew. He would be annoyed that she'd caught him off-guard. They had a deal and this wasn't part of it.

At least, it hasn't been up to now, said a voice in her head. *But things change.*

She recalled how often Charlie had accused her of being devoted to facts, figures and logic.

'You simply never give in,' he'd said, as though it were a crime.

'No, I don't give in. I like to win, and I'm going to win this time, whatever I have to do, and however long it takes.'

She looked down at Damiano's face lying sideways on the pillow, eyes closed, completely unaware of her.

'I'm going to win,' she murmured softly. 'You wait and see.'

She'd said, *'Whatever I have to do,'* and that meant being prepared to take risks. Now she decided on the first risk.

Moving slowly, she leaned down and let her lips brush against his cheek. He didn't open his eyes but she thought he murmured something. Crossing her fingers, she kissed his cheek again, then quickly slid out of bed and went to the window, turning so that she could see the moment when he awoke, and the way his eyes instinctively looked at her side of the bed. Now empty.

She reached up to stretch in the sunlight, yawning just loud enough to catch his attention.

'Good morning,' he said.

She glanced at him with eyebrows raised as though surprised to find him there.

'Good morning,' she replied. 'Oh, isn't it a lovely day?' She yawned again, turning this way and that, so that the sun illuminated the silk nightdress and the way it lay against her slim figure.

'Did you have a good night?' he asked politely.

'Lovely. I slept like a log, which I really needed because yesterday was so exhausting. What about you?'

'The same,' he said.

It wasn't true. He'd lain awake for a long time, keeping a careful distance between them, listening to her breathing, alert for the slightest difference in the sound. But he heard nothing he could interpret as encouragement to reach out to her.

Nor would there be, he realised. She had declared her freedom from love in words that could not have been plainer.

But frustration was new to him and he knew he coped with it badly. In the last moments of sleep he'd been tormented by a fantasy in which she'd dropped a tender kiss on his face. But when he awoke she wasn't with him but standing by the window, lost in thoughts that he guessed had nothing to do with himself. He'd assumed a casual air, but it had been hard.

'I suppose we should get up,' he said.

At breakfast Pietro was bubbling with ideas for showing Sally around Venice, starting with a ride in a gondola. She was eager for this. Damiano had taken her in a gondola when he proposed, but that had been a dark night. Now she wanted to enjoy the light.

'I don't understand,' she said as they glided along. 'There's only one oarsman, so you'd think the gondola would go round in circles. How come it's moving in a straight line?'

'Because it's bigger on one side than the other,' Pietro explained.

He pointed out how the gondola bulged wider on the oarsman's side, slowing the water down, so that the movement of the oar simply made the two sides of equal speed. Despite his youth he had an authoritative manner, and Sally listened with interest.

'You're a real expert,' she said admiringly.

'I'm a Venetian,' Pietro said, as though that explained everything.

Which it did, Sally appreciated.

'Yes, of course,' she said warmly. 'You must tell me a lot more.'

She was already on splendid terms with the child, and nothing could have made things better than her willingness to listen while he explained things about the city like a teacher instructing a student.

They spent the weekend in each other's company, but there was a pause when Monday came and he had to attend school. Damiano's time was taken up with his business interests and Sally, 'the great organiser' was faced with the problem of organising her new life.

'I've got to learn Italian,' she told Damiano. 'I can speak English with everyone in this house, but outside I'm at a disadvantage. And disadvantage is something I cannot live with.'

'How did I know you were going to say that?' he said appreciatively. 'Would I be accused of trying to control you if I suggested a good teacher?'

'I'll thump you if you don't,' she said, aiming a pretend punch at him, much to the enjoyment of Pietro, who was watching.

The teacher he suggested was excellent. After a few lessons Sally insisted that Charlie join her.

'Must I?' he protested. 'I'm doing all right in the hotel. Everyone speaks English.'

'That's not enough. You've got to become an expert.'

'Do as she tells you, Charlie,' Damiano broke in. 'Or she might thump you and, believe me, you don't want that.'

He rubbed his face as he spoke. When they were alone Sally confronted him.

'That's taking it beyond a joke. Now he'll think I really do thump you.'

'You did, last night,' he said. 'For some reason you slept restlessly, flailing your arms about like a demented windmill. I reached out, meaning to awaken you, and your hand caught my face. Nearly knocked me out.'

'I'm sorry. Why didn't you wake me?'

'Are you kidding? I fled for my life. Look.'

He turned his head so that she could see a slight bruise near the hairline.

'I did that?' she asked, aghast. 'I swear I never meant to.'

'I know.' He grinned. 'Some people just go through life knocking people out without realising it. But I can suffer in silence.'

'Thank you. It's nice of you to see the funny side.'

It was a relief to be able to dismiss it as a joke, but in her heart she knew there was a reason for her restless sleep. It grew from lying next to Damiano, aching for his touch, trembling with the frustration of knowing that he would keep his distance. In sleep the tension didn't leave her. It merely transmuted into nightmares.

But she would learn to cope, she assured herself. It was easy to believe that she could succeed since she was increasingly at home in their daily life. Damiano might not pursue her with passion, but in other respects his admiration for her was growing.

One morning she entered his office to find him frowning over a paper filled with figures.

'Just a moment,' he asked edgily. 'This stuff is going to give me a nervous breakdown.'

She looked over his shoulder at the column of figures where his finger was pointing.

'Can't you use this here?' she asked, pointing to another column. 'I don't know exactly what they refer to but they make a much more impressive result than the ones over there.'

'They look about the same to me,' he said.

'At first sight, yes, they do. But they add up differently. They come to much more, if that helps.'

'It certainly would if—' He seized a calculator and began to hit keys. At last he stopped and stared at her. 'You're right. But how did you know that?'

'I added them up.'

'In your head?'

'It's a trick I've always had. I read figures and my brain adds them automatically. Why do you think I became an accountant? It's the only thing I'm good at.'

'Good at?' he exclaimed with a touch of awe. 'I thought I was good at figures but I can't do that.'

'So what? Adding them up in a moment is little more than a circus trick. What matters is knowing what to do with the results when you have them. That's what makes you a great businessman.'

'I see you're playing the tactful wife,' Damiano said with a grin. 'Don't let your husband feel small because you can do something he can't.'

'Well, I've been made to suffer for it over time. I performed that "circus trick" for a boyfriend once, and never saw him again. He was a fellow student on my accountancy course so I thought I was safe.'

'Showing you were more talented than him was the death knell of your relationship.'

'Aha! Will it be the death knell of ours?'

'Not at all. You've just shown me another way I can make use of you, and I'm going to make the most of it.' He raised his glass. *Salute!*'

'*Salute!*' she responded, raising her own. Smiling, they clinked glasses.

There were several dinner invitations, for everyone wanted to meet Damiano's wife. She found that she was fast acquiring a reputation as a woman to be reckoned with. One evening she fell into conversation with an influential elderly man who had been a university professor. The talk turned to masks and the way the fluid changing of personalities typified Venice.

'But I think my own country can claim a little credit as well,' she observed.

'England?' the old man echoed as though the mere idea was preposterous.

'Well, the English did produce William Shakespeare, who wrote the line, "One man in his time plays many parts." I think we knew something about it too.'

'Hmm,' the old man said wryly. 'I suppose I have to concede that.'

'Of course,' she added, 'it's always possible that Shakespeare was secretly a Venetian.'

'Of course he was! That settles it.'

Cheers and laughter went around the table. Nods were exchanged as everyone understood why Damiano had chosen this lively, intelligent lady.

Looking across the table, she saw that once again he was raising his glass to her. She returned the gesture, conscious that the other guests were watching them, envying a couple in such perfect accord.

Not yet, she thought with a little sigh. Not yet. But one day. Soon.

* * *

Pietro took his role as guide seriously.

'It'll soon be time for the *Su e Zo per i Ponti*,' he told her. 'You'll enjoy that.'

'We all will,' Mario announced.

'But what is it?' she wanted to know.

'It's a race "Up and Down the Bridges",' Mario explained. 'It starts in the Piazza San Marco. You're given a map of places to tick off as you reach them and you have to cross about fifty-six bridges to get to the end, which is San Marco again. All the profits go to charity.'

'It also has a touch of *bacarada*,' Damiano observed, amused. 'You'd probably call that a pub crawl. Not surprisingly it's very popular, so I dare say you'll be taking part, Mario.'

'You bet.'

'And me,' Charlie chimed in.

The following Sunday they all gathered in the Piazza to cheer Mario and Charlie on their way. Although Carnival was over its spirit could still be felt, and many of the runners were in theatrical costumes. Mario was again dressed as Arlecchino, which Sally observed seemed to suit him well.

'You think that's all there is to me?' Mario queried softly.

'No, I'm sure there's much more to you,' she

said, 'and any day now the right girl will bring it out.'

'The right girl, yes. But maybe—ah, well.'

'What does "ah, well" mean? All the girls love you,' she teased.

'Not quite all of them.'

He said it with a glance at her that once she might have interpreted as flirtation. It wasn't the first time Mario had spoken thus, but she always brushed these moments aside, assuring herself that Mario saw himself as her kid brother. Nothing more.

'You're right,' she said jokingly. 'Some girls must be put off by your serious, intellectual nature.'

'You're making fun of me, aren't you?'

'However did you guess?' She chuckled and turned away to leave the room.

'Sally,' he called.

She turned back. There was an uneasy look on his face that she'd never seen before.

'What is it, Mario?'

'It's just that—if things had been different—'

'If things had been different I'd never have met Damiano, and that would have been a great pity.'

'Does he make you happy?'

'Why don't you ask him if I make him happy?' she said lightly. 'That's the important thing.'

'And Charlie? You did it for him, didn't you?

Sally—' Suddenly his voice was serious. 'Do you ever do anything for yourself?'

'Everything. I'm the most selfish creature in creation. Ah, good, there's Charlie.' She could barely keep the relief out of her voice.

It felt strange to be dismissing Mario so lightly. Once the admiration of a good-looking young man would have delighted her. But now everything in the world had changed. Only Damiano existed.

She wasn't in love with him, she assured herself. That would be a disaster. But he was rightfully hers and she was determined to claim her property.

Charlie was also dressed as a clown, and fizzing with anticipation. Sally, Damiano and Pietro waved him and Mario off from St Mark's and wandered through the city, keeping the runners in view as much as possible. Hours later the lads joined them, cheering and slightly the worse for wear. There was a riotous family supper, after which they strolled home through the streets.

All around them were flashes of light as people took photographs of the jolly crowd. Charlie and Mario danced along, accompanied by Pietro, who waved at everyone. Damiano walked with his arm around Sally's shoulder and her arm about his waist.

'It was a good day, wasn't it?' he said.

'Oh, yes, it was lovely,' she said, turning her head to look up and meet his warm smile.

He tightened his arm, looking more closely into her face. For a moment she thought he would kiss her, but a blinding flash made her tense, covering her eyes.

'Ow!' she said. 'Where did that come from?'

'Up there,' he said, pointing.

They looked up at an open window, but there was no longer anybody to be seen.

'Never mind,' Damiano said. 'It probably wasn't us they were trying to get a shot of, but those mad boys.'

The lads were having the time of their lives, and Sally laughed with pleasure at the sight of them. It was the happiest day she'd spent for a while, and she wondered if the night could be happier yet.

But when they reached home Damiano said, 'You're half asleep. Go to bed. I'll be up in a while.'

'Mmm,' she said, realising that he was right, and she was already nodding off. When he came to bed an hour later she was dead to the world.

Next morning Mario and Charlie were full of stories about their crazy antics. Pietro cheered them on, Toby wuffed his agreement and Damiano grinned with pleasure, occasionally meeting Sally's eyes in a look of family solidarity.

He was due to visit another of his Venetian hotels that morning, and when he invited her to come with him she gladly accepted. They walked there and back, cheerful in the sunshine that was taking over the city. Sally was dazed by the narrow winding canals that stretched all around them like a maze. At last a spirit of mischief made her dart away from Damiano, out of sight. She heard him following and slipped around the next corner.

Then she realised that she'd made a mistake, having come so far that she was lost.

'Give in?' said a voice behind her.

It was Damiano, who'd taken a short cut to trick her, and now stood there grinning as he put both arms about her so that she was effectively imprisoned against his chest.

'You'll tease me once too often,' he growled.

'I wonder what will happen then.'

'You may soon find out. This way.'

He led her into the next alley, where there was a little café. There he ordered coffee, not taking his hand from her, and finally sitting down between her and the door.

'I thought you'd find me sooner than that,' she said, half gasping, half laughing. 'You know this town so much better than me.'

'I like to think I do, but nobody really knows

Venice as well as they think they do. It's a city of secrets, and these tiny, narrow alleys are a kind of symbol of that. You're at home here. I've felt that from the start.'

'Well, I certainly love it.'

'I mean more than that. Deep inside yourself you are as mysterious as Venice. One day you will have a secret to conceal from me, and I know you'll do so with great skill.'

'But why should I ever conceal a secret from you?'

'You'll know that when the time comes.' He leaned back a little and considered her. 'Nature has made you a Venetian at heart, and fate has brought you home.'

It was a charming speech, full of a welcome and acceptance that warmed her heart. If only, she thought, there had been just a hint of something more, something she might tell herself was love rather than merely kindness.

A young couple came drifting towards them along the alley. They held each other tightly, faces close, not looking where they were going, indifferent to their surroundings as long as they had each other. The man was speaking words that she could just hear.

'Te vojo ben...te vojo ben.'

Whatever the words meant they gave the girl great joy. Her face lit up and she pressed herself more tightly against him.

'What language are they talking?' Sally asked. 'It doesn't sound like Italian.'

'It isn't. It's Venetian dialect.'

'What does *Te vojo ben* mean?'

'Literally it means "I wish you well", but it's the Venetian way of saying "I love you".'

'I love you,' she murmured.

She didn't look at him as she spoke. He might have read in her eyes that she was doing more than merely reciting the words. But he only said, 'Yes, that's it,' like a schoolmaster encouraging a pupil who was doing well.

He put an arm about her shoulder. 'Come along. Time to go home.'

At home a shock awaited her. Nora was there, looking concerned.

'This was put through the door,' she said, indicating an envelope on which was written *'Signora Ferrone'*.

Sally took it into the garden, where she tore it open, and stared at what she found.

There was a photograph taken last night, showing her and Damiano walking together, presenting a picture of a happy couple. With it was a handwritten note.

You think you're winning, don't you? I'll bet he didn't tell you that it's Gina's birthday next week. Imelda

There was no doubt of Imelda's meaning. She was spitefully warning Sally that this would be a sacred day for Damiano, and she should be prepared to be tossed into the background while he thought only of his true love.

Her heart was beating harder. The mere name Gina could have that effect, and it grew worse when she read a final sentence scribbled on the note.

PS He's always visited her grave and spent the day weeping over it. I wonder what he'll do this year. Perhaps he'll be different with you. Or perhaps not.

No, he wouldn't be different, Sally told herself bitterly. Gina was still there in Damiano's heart. She'd always known that, and told herself she'd accepted it. But now she was stunned by the power it still had to hurt.

Which was exactly what Imelda had intended.

She studied the photograph again, remembering how the flashing light had startled her the night before. That must have been Imelda, taking this picture. Which meant she was following them, spying, infuriated by their appearance of happiness, and determined to destroy it.

And she could succeed, Sally thought in sudden fear.

She had the sense of standing at a crossroads. The decision she made now would affect everything that came afterwards.

But she wasn't going to let herself be bullied by Imelda, and Damiano was the strongest ally she could have. Bracing herself, she headed for his office.

He looked up in surprise as she entered.

'Has something upset you? Nothing I've done, I hope.'

'Yes, something's upset me, but it's not you. It's Imelda. She's written to me about Gina's birthday, obviously trying to cause trouble.'

She handed him the papers, and watched as he grew pale and closed his eyes.

'I'm sorry,' he said. 'You shouldn't have found out like this. I meant to tell you but I didn't know how, and I kept putting it off.'

'So she's right about you visiting the grave?'

She didn't add, 'And weeping over it.' But the words seemed to hang in the air.

'Yes. It's as much for Pietro as myself. The first birthday after her death I took him there so that we could all be together on her birthday. After that we visited her every year. It means a lot to him.'

'And you,' Sally forced herself to say. 'You told me once before that you still talk to her.'

'I told you that? Yes, I did. I remember.' She

could see that he'd forgotten how easily he'd confided in her from the start, and the memory startled him.

What else had he forgotten? she wondered. What did he try to forget? Or did he not try?

'Damn Imelda!' he growled glancing at the papers. 'She hated my going there, especially with Pietro. She tried to stop us.'

'That's dreadful. He's got the right to visit his mother.'

'So you won't mind if I go, and take him with me?'

She hesitated a moment before asking quietly, 'What does it matter if I mind or not?'

'What does it—? Of course it matters. You're my wife.'

Not really, she thought. But she didn't say it aloud.

He said uneasily, 'I was afraid you might feel— well—'

Sally made a quick decision. Her next words were spoken from behind a mask of light-hearted good humour, almost indifference.

'But we've always talked openly about Gina. I know she's still important to you and Pietro, and I wouldn't interfere. Of course you must take him to her. They belong to each other.'

'Belong to each other,' he echoed slowly. 'Do you remember, when we'd just met, I said you must be the kindest person in the world? I was right. The kindest and most understanding. There's nothing better I could have done for Pietro than bring you into the family.' He gave a reflective smile, aimed partly at her but partly at his inner self. 'Yes, Gina still belongs to him, but now you belong to him too. And he's beginning to belong to you.'

'I hope so. I love him dearly. When you visit Gina, can I come too?'

He gazed at her in disbelief. 'You'd do that?'

'Of course. If I'm part of the family then I have to be part of this. But if you don't want me—'

'Yes, I want you,' he said quickly.

'Then it's up to Pietro. He may not like the idea.'

'Of course he will.'

He was right. Not only was Pietro glad of her coming but he seemed surprised that there had ever been a doubt. Sally was his mother now, and of course she would join him on a family expedition. He said little, but the way he squeezed her hand spoke volumes.

When she was alone with Damiano she said, 'What would you have done if I hadn't found out?'

'Do you mean would I have slipped away without telling you? No. That would have meant lying to you and I couldn't do that. I'd have told you

about it. I've been trying to pluck up the courage, but I guess I don't have that much courage.'

'You don't need courage with me,' she pointed
out.

'No, I'm beginning to understand that.'

CHAPTER ELEVEN

WHEN THE DAY came she awoke to find Damiano standing at the window, lost in thought. After a moment he looked up at the sky.

'How is the weather?' she asked.

'Better now, thank goodness. Spring is here.'

As they ate breakfast Nora came to announce that a man had come with a delivery of flowers. As Damiano was inspecting them his driver appeared to say that the motor boat was ready. Pietro headed for the door with Toby.

'Toby's allowed to come,' Damiano explained. 'As long as he's kept on a lead and behaves himself.'

The cemetery was on the island of San Michele, out in the lagoon. Soon they were heading out across the water. At last the island came into view, and a few minutes later they drew up at the landing bay.

She thought San Michele was one of the most beautiful places she had ever seen. Pietro eagerly took her hand and led her down a path to where the headstones rose from the grass.

As she'd expected Gina's grave was adorned with her photograph. It was almost life size, with a glowing smile for everyone who visited her.

She stood back to let Pietro approach his mother alone. He laid flowers on the ground and chatted to her eagerly, pointing at Sally in a way that made it clear he was introducing her.

'He talks to her as though she was still alive,' she murmured to Damiano as he came to stand beside her. 'But I suppose in a way she is.'

'Yes. I remember feeling that the first time I came here, with Pietro. She'd been dead only a few weeks, and I wanted to show her our baby so that we could enjoy him together. That sounds mad, doesn't it? How could we enjoy anything together when she was dead?'

'But she was still alive in your heart. If you felt that the two of you were together, then you were. And you still are.'

He turned her to face him, looking closely into her face. 'How can you of all people say that?'

'Because it's true. You're still a couple and Pietro knows it.'

'But he's got you now.'

'Yes, but I'm not instead of Gina. I'm as well as Gina. All of us together are a family. You, me, Pietro—' she gave a little laugh '—and Toby.'

Something in his expression told her that he was confused, searching for the right words. Before he could speak Pietro returned from the grave, looking happy.

'She likes you,' he said.

'I like her. In fact I've brought her something.'

From her bag she took out the small posy that she'd bought the previous day, and went to lay it beside Pietro's offering.

She had an impulse to speak to Gina, but before she could do so she heard a squeak of dismay behind her. Looking back, she saw that Toby had escaped and was running away with Pietro chasing after him. She joined in the chase, managing to head him off and seize him before he went too far.

'Sorry,' Pietro said, catching up. 'He just wriggled free and dashed off.'

'I'll bet he's good at seizing his chance,' she said. 'Come on, let's go.'

They turned back in the direction of the grave, but as they neared it she drew a sharp breath. Damiano was there, kneeling before the headstone, his eyes fixed on Gina's picture, and an expression that caused Sally a shaft of pain. He was not weeping, as Imelda had predicted, but there was despair and misery in his face.

She could see his lips moving, but not make out what he was saying. As she watched he lowered his head and reached out to touch the picture. When he lifted his head again he was still speaking, and she thought she could make out the words, 'I'm sorry—I'm so sorry.'

She wanted to cry out. She'd deluded herself that Damiano was becoming hers, but now he was apologising to Gina for his marriage, which he clearly felt was a betrayal.

Pietro hadn't noticed his father. His attention was taken by Toby, playing up again. By the time he'd got the dog under control Damiano was waiting for them, a fixed smile on his face.

'Are we ready to go?' he asked. 'I've added the flowers. Sally, that was a charming posy you left her.'

He'd changed his mask very skilfully, she thought. The grieving husband had been set aside, replaced by a sensible man who knew the correct thing to say. Now she must don a similar mask.

'It was an act of friendship,' she said. 'I know she'll like that.'

'I'm sure she will.'

They headed for the bay but when they were nearly there Sally came to a sudden decision.

'Oh, goodness!' she said, clutching her pocket. 'I dropped something back there. I must go and fetch it.'

She ran away before they could reply. In fact

she hadn't dropped anything. The story was an excuse to return to Gina's grave alone.

'You knew I'd be back, didn't you?' she said as soon as she arrived. She moved close so that she could look directly into Gina's eyes.

'The little time you had must have been wonderful for you both. Then you lost each other, and you lost Pietro. But trust me. I love him and I'll always be good to him. You must know Pietro is safe with me. And Damiano too. He'll always come first. I'll try to be everything he wants, and give him whatever he needs.

'I saw him here with you a few minutes ago, and everything he feels was there in his face. He tried to hide it from me, but he couldn't. I know he still loves you, and he always will. You must have been the best wife in the world to have made him so happy that he can never forget you. Perhaps one day he'll come to love me a little, but I'll never take your place.'

Overhead the trees rustled in the growing wind. She looked up at the branches swaying, almost as though something had agitated them. Glancing back at Gina, she had the strange feeling that all was not well with her.

'It's all right,' she told her. 'You'll always come first with him. I have to accept that, but I can't pretend it doesn't hurt. And in time it will hurt more, unless—can that happen? Dare I hope for it?'

She backed away, still watching the beautiful, fascinating face, whose eyes seemed to follow her. She tried to understand that look, to read into it the bond of trust that she had tried to establish between them. But there was something else, something she didn't understand, and which made her shiver.

'What is it?' she said urgently. 'What are you trying to tell me? Because there's something I don't know, isn't there?'

But the wind died and the branches overhead fell silent, leaving her in a bleak and empty desert.

Silence. Nothing.

She had a sudden, desperate need to get away from this place. She hurried back to the others.

'All right?' Damiano asked as she joined him. 'Did you find what you'd lost?'

'Oh, yes, I found it.' She couldn't help adding, 'I found a great deal.'

He gave her a curious look but asked no questions, which was lucky. Even to herself she would have found it hard to describe the thoughts and sensations that possessed her.

A realisation was creeping up on her. Needing more time alone to brood on it, she went to bed early. Damiano pleaded work before he could retire, but he accompanied her to their room.

'You were wonderful today,' he said. 'You did

everything right, as you always do. I'm the luckiest man alive because I have you, and your kindness.'

He put his arms about her, drawing her close so that her head was against his shoulder.

'Thank you,' he said. 'Thank you with all my heart.'

She wrapped her arms around his body, loving the feeling that he wanted to be close to her.

'You don't have to thank me,' she said. 'We made a deal and I'm keeping my side.'

'You're giving more than that, far more than we agreed, or I ever hoped for.'

Her heart missed a beat. Had he begun to suspect why she gave so much more than he expected? Could she take the chance?

'Damiano—'

'Come on, time for you to get some rest.' He withdrew his arms, forcing her to do the same. He opened the bedroom door. 'I'll come in quietly later, not to awaken you.'

Then he was gone and she had the solitude she needed to consider the revelation that had taken hold of her today.

Seeing Damiano with Gina, his face devastated by grief for her, had been a turning point. It was as though a brilliant light had suddenly illuminated all that had happened since the day they had met. Now she could see and understand everything she had refused to face before.

I'm in love with him, she thought. I have been almost from the start.

The magic had always been there. Wary of love, she'd fought it, refusing to recognise how devastating was his effect on her. But with every touch, every smile, he had invaded her heart, refusing to be banished.

Why had she never faced the truth before? The physical excitement that no other man had been able to inspire in her had sprung to life at Damiano's touch. She'd ignored it, fearful of being vulnerable, something she had always tried never to be. The way he kept his distance had maddened her more and more, until she had to face the fact that she wanted him in her bed, and that desire could be a signpost on the road to love.

Mysteriously Gina seemed to be with her again, invisible but powerful, throwing down a challenge. And Sally's defiant spirit arose.

'From now on everything is going to be different. He was yours once, but he's mine now.'

She recalled a conversation she'd had with Charlie when, as so often before, he'd tried to wriggle out of blame for his own irresponsibility by despising her ease with facts and figures.

'You haven't got a heart,' he'd accused. 'You're just calculating.'

'If by calculating you mean I make sensible plans, then I plead guilty.'

And I've got a plan now, she thought. Oh, yes, I've got a plan and I'm going to make it work. And if that makes me calculating, then I'll calculate, because so much is at stake. All the happiness I could ever know, now and for the rest of my life. That's what I'm gambling for, and if the odds are high I'll just have to gamble harder. And then harder. Until I win.

'And I'm going to win.'

Pietro was eager to tell Sally that soon there would be another festival, the Feast of St Mark.

'There's a gondola race,' he said. 'And people hold dances in the evening. Papa always has one in the hotel, and there's a lot of soppy stuff.'

'What kind of soppy stuff?' she asked.

'It's also known as *La Festa del Boccolo*,' said Mario, who'd been listening with amusement. '*Boccolo* means rosebud. There's a story about a man who fell in love with a noble woman hundreds of years ago. He was only a servant so he couldn't hope to marry her in those days. He joined the army and was killed in action. Before he died he plucked a rosebud and sent it back to her. Supposedly it was stained with his blood, so they still use red ones today.'

'What a sad story,' she mused.

'It's soppy,' said Pietro contemptuously. 'Come on, Toby, let's go and play.'

'That's not like him,' Sally observed when the boy and his dog had gone.

'Children sometimes give rosebuds to their mothers,' Mario said. 'He did it once, with Imelda. She seemed to receive it more or less well, but then she threw it away. He found it a couple of days later.'

'I'd like to slap her,' Sally said crossly.

'I think Pietro might give you a rosebud this time. He's closer to you than he ever was to Imelda. Damiano's over the moon about what a great mother you are.'

'It's nice to know that he approves of me,' Sally said in a voice that gave nothing away.

She promised herself that when she was finished he would do more than approve of her for being a good mother to his son. He would desire her as passionately as she desired him. If she wasn't there he would be desolate. His heart would beat for her and her alone, not only with desire, but with love.

This was her plan. The time was coming when she would don a new mask, but there were things still to be decided.

She slipped away to the shop where Mario had taken her to buy what she needed for Carnival. After inspecting everything closely she found exactly what she wanted: a glamorous costume and an intriguing mask.

She managed to carry everything home without being discovered, and hurried upstairs, hiding her purchases away in her old room until the moment she would need them.

That came with the Festival of St Mark. The day started well, with Damiano presenting her with a small bouquet of red rosebuds over breakfast. Pietro gave her a rosebud of his own, then exchanged a smile and a nod with his father. Charlie and Mario applauded.

'Come on,' Pietro said excitedly when breakfast was over. 'Time for the gondola race.'

They secured places in a building overlooking the canal and cheered as a gondolier attached to the hotel won the race by a length. Then everyone streamed back for the celebrations, and to prepare for the masked ball in the evening.

'Fine, I'll wear what I wore before,' Sally declared. 'What about you?'

'The same.'

They dressed together. She put on the gold satin garment she'd bought for last time and he helped her with the buttons. Her heart was beating as the moment drew near when she must put her plan into action. Suddenly she closed her eyes and clutched her head.

'What is it?' he asked anxiously.

'Just a headache. I thought it would have gone by now, but it's getting worse.'

'Are you sure you're well enough for tonight?'

'Not really. Would you mind if I didn't go?'

'If you're not well I'd rather you stayed here.'

'Then I will.'

With his help she stripped off the dress and lay down. He kissed her cheek and departed.

The plan had begun.

She lay still to give him time to leave. When she was sure he was gone she slipped out and down the corridor to her own room. There she hurriedly dressed in an elegant red and blue gown she'd bought for tonight. The mask was glamorous, glittering about the eyes and covering most of her face with just a small gap for her mouth. A man looking down at her would just be able to see her smile, but no more.

She removed her wedding ring and put it away. Nobody must see it tonight. Until now the ring had been almost meaningless but that was going to change.

As she slipped out into the corridor the house was silent. Charlie and Mario were out having fun. Pietro was already asleep. The housekeeper remained at home for his sake but she was out of sight in the kitchen as Sally hurried down the stairs and slipped through the connecting door to the hotel.

At once she was in a crowd of revellers and was able to make her way to the ballroom without attracting notice.

As soon as she entered she looked for Damiano. It was hard because the ballroom lights were kept low, increasing the dramatic atmosphere. She had to search before she found him. His back was to her, but he wore the black velvet suit. She edged towards him, then halted with shock.

He was holding a woman close to him, his right hand stroking her neck, then drifting down to caress her breasts, his fingers easing their way into the material.

So that was it! That was what his restraint amounted to. He didn't need to sleep with her because he was fooling around with other women. She wanted to scream, run away, fly at him, tear off his mask and slap his face.

If only she could decide which.

But while she was still struggling with temptation, the man moved so that his left hand came into view, and suddenly all questions were answered.

Damiano had a scar on the back of his left hand, and she was just close enough to see that this man had no such scar. This wasn't him, but a man wearing a very similar costume.

For a moment she was dizzy with relief as the nightmares that had danced before her faded. But where was he? She must identify him quickly without further mistakes. She glided through the crowd, frantically searching.

She saw him at last. The mask covered most of his face but he was holding up a glass of wine high enough for her to just make out the scar.

Now things were working out well. For her plan to succeed they must each recognise the other, but pretend otherwise, at least at the start.

Time for action.

He glanced in her direction and she seized a glass from a passing waiter, holding it up, approaching him to clink glasses, then turning away again.

'Wait!' He detained her with a hand on her arm. 'You're surely not going to leave me just like that.'

'Aren't I?' she said in a teasing voice. 'I just came to say hello.'

'Hello. Not goodbye.'

'Perhaps. Perhaps not. I have other hellos to say.' She indicated a group of men nearby.

He moved closer. 'Let me see if I can change your mind about that.'

Taking her glass, he set it aside with his own, and slid a hand around her waist.

'Hello,' he said.

She smiled. 'Hello.'

As they glided around the floor he held her too

close for propriety. Looking up, she found his mouth close to hers, the lips touched with a faint smile that might have been designed to tempt her.

Had he recognised her? Did he think he was dancing with a stranger? Or did he suspect the truth and was trying to decide? Of the three she decided the third would be the most intriguing.

'Who are you?' he murmured.

She made her laugh as teasing as possible.

'Come, come, you're a Venetian. You know that I'm everybody and nobody. And does it really matter which?'

'It does to me.'

She laughed again. 'If you don't know who I really am, it's because you're afraid to know.'

She said the last words with great significance, and felt his clasp tighten.

'Why should I be afraid?' he asked.

'Only you can answer that. Some things we don't know because we don't want to know them.'

'You make me sound like a coward.'

'Not a coward, just a man like every other man on earth.'

'So you despise us all?'

'No, but I watch you with caution.'

He was silent for a moment. Then suddenly he said, 'I know another woman who does that. She too has things she doesn't want to know.'

'About herself, or about you?'

'Both, I suspect. And I can't decide whether to tell her.'

'But do you know her secrets?'

'I know secrets she doesn't suspect.'

'Perhaps it's the same with her.'

'I often think it is,' he said in a low voice.

The waltz came to an end, and she drew away from him. She needed time to think. Damiano's words sounded as though he saw past her mask to the woman within. Deep inside some instinct told her that they were talking a secret language known only to the two of them.

'Dance with me again,' he said. 'Dance with me *now*.'

'Not now. Later, when I'm ready.'

She turned and departed before he could become more demanding. Other admirers clamoured for her attention and she went through them one by one, conscious of Damiano keeping her under permanent observation, until at last he stepped in and reclaimed her.

'My turn,' he said, taking firm hold and guiding her onto the dance floor. After a few turns he said, 'You haven't told me your name.'

But he had recognised her. She was confident of that now. A strange and exciting chance had opened before her. They could talk openly, yet behind the protection of their masks. It sounded impossible, but in the magical air of Venice nothing was really impossible.

'Your name,' he repeated.

'I have several names. Tonight I am Mysteria, the woman of many masks. Haven't you sensed that already?'

'Perhaps. Maybe I don't know whether to believe it. It's so confusing.'

She gave a soft laugh, calculated to entice him.

'If it's confusing, that's a reason to believe it.'

'Now you're trying to confuse me even more.'

'Why would I want to do that?'

He had danced her into a corner, turning her so that she was shielded from everyone.

'Kiss me,' he commanded.

'In these masks? Impossible.'

He tightened his grip but it was, as she said, impossible to get close enough.

'Do I know you?' he breathed. 'Are you— could you be—?'

'I could be anyone you want me to be. But who do you want?'

'I want—I want—*you!*'

'But I am nobody. I don't exist.'

'Don't say that.'

'After tonight we will never meet again. I will vanish into thin air. That other woman will still be there, and you'll have to decide if we're the same person. And you will wonder if we ever met.' She gave a slight chuckle. 'You'll probably feel that it's best if we didn't.'

'Why do you laugh at me? Does it amuse you to confuse me?'

'Yes,' she admitted. 'A man is always amusing when he's at a disadvantage.'

'Damn you!' he whispered.

Before he could say or do more someone called his name. Furiously he turned to them, forcing himself to engage in polite conversation. When he turned back she had gone.

Watching him from the doorway, Sally could see his air of desperation as he looked this way and that. At last he grew close enough to see her, and came to a sudden sharp halt.

Sally raised her hand and beckoned to him, retreating through the open doorway. He followed fast, catching up, gazing down at her, breathing heavily.

'Where are you going?' he demanded.

'Wherever you want to take me. I wonder where that could be.'

'You know where it is. I'm taking you where you belong, to my room, to my bed. Unless—' His confidence seemed to weaken. 'Unless you do not wish to go there with me.'

She smiled. 'Do you think that is my wish?'

'I don't know what I think. I don't know anything about anything any more.'

'Then why don't we find out?' She indicated the way ahead. 'Go on, lead me. After all, you're in command. You lead, I follow.'

What little she could see of his mouth twisted wryly. 'We both know that's not true.'

'Who could possibly dictate to you?'

'There is one woman who could.'

'Lead on.'

She held out her hand. He took it and led the way through the hotel until they reached the connecting door. In a moment they were through and on their way up to the bedroom.

Sally had a blissful sensation that fate had blessed her plans. Everything was going well. She had no doubt that Damiano had recognised her.

He knew this was Sally, but which Sally? How many might there be? Her disguise had freed them both from the prison of their usual selves. Now they could each make love to a 'stranger' without being faithless to each other.

As they entered their bedroom he reached out to the wall switch, but she restrained him.

'No,' she murmured. 'We don't need light.'

After a moment he nodded. 'I don't need to see you,' he agreed.

'And why should you want to? You already know the things that matter about me.' She moved closer so that he could feel her breath against his mouth. 'Otherwise you wouldn't be here.'

'And you?' he asked. 'Don't you want to know who I am?'

'But I do know who you are. You're the man who came when I beckoned.'

'Does every man come at your command?'

For answer she gave a soft chuckle. 'What do you think?'

'I think every man follows you because he can't help himself.'

'What do the others matter? What does anything matter except that we are here, now, together?'

She stripped off her own mask, then reached up to his and slowly pulled it away. In the semi darkness she could just see his face enough to be sure it was Damiano, and knew he could see hers. But for the moment they should keep silent about their mutual recognition and enjoy the advantages of strangers.

She touched his mouth lightly with her fingertips, and would have drawn them away but he seized her hand, pressing it against his lips, kissing it again and again. Her response was a soft chuckle.

'Why are you laughing?' he demanded. 'Was that what you meant me to do? Am I dancing to your tune?'

'Do you think you are?'

'I don't know,' he said hoarsely.

'Would you mind?'

After a long moment he whispered, 'No.'

'I think you would. No man likes a woman to have too much power.'

'That depends how she uses her power.'

She gave a soft laugh. 'No, it doesn't. No woman can be trusted. Never forget that.'

'Do you say that I shouldn't trust you?'

'That's your decision. If you take the risk of trusting me—I can do as I like.'

'Stop it,' he said hoarsely. 'Stop trying to turn me against you.'

'But you can always send me away. You're the one in control now. Aren't you?'

'Yes,' he said, but his voice shook.

'Just throw me out, say you never want to see me again, and I'll—'

The last words were silenced by his mouth on hers. It was what she'd wanted but she was still taken by surprise. The force and urgency of his kiss told of a man driven to the edge of control, ready to step into uncharted waters.

Excitement rose in her. She too was venturing into uncharted waters and this was a journey they would take together.

As he kissed her his hands began to move over her body, pulling at the laces that fixed her dress, pushing it from her shoulders until at last it fell to the floor. She responded by working on his coat, helping him wrench it off. As if given a signal he seized her up in his arms and strode to the bed.

'Is this our fate?' she whispered. 'Are you set on imposing your will on me?'

'I impose nothing.' There was a tinge of anger in his voice. 'I'm doing what you always meant me to do, and we both know it.'

'I'm not sure that I do know it. You might have to persuade me.'

'Right.' His mouth was on hers again, forceful but caressing at the same time, sending excitement pulsing through her so strongly that she could barely stand. She moved her own lips against him, seeking to inspire him with thrills as great as her own, sensing his reaction in the trembling of his body.

She had longed for this, dreamed of it. Now she seemed possessed by something beyond herself. Victory was in her grasp and she must seize it before the chance slipped away. She wasn't sure who it was who ripped open his shirt buttons. It might have been herself, but the action held more of the other self who had taken her over.

That other Sally ran her hands over his bare chest, relishing the feel of his muscles, his smooth skin, the tension of desire that throbbed through him.

Now she was naked, and so was he. It was too dark to see but she could feel the length of his body against her, feel the caresses that seemed to invade her everywhere, until at last he took possession of her completely, and the whole world changed.

A long gasp broke from her as she sensed first the power of his desire, then her own uncontrollable response. For a few moments madness consumed them both, and they clung to each other, seeking pleasure and comfort in the same moments.

For Sally it was as though everything had been drained from her. She was no longer herself but a new woman, open to the world, to this man, to a wealth of new experiences and joys waiting to be discovered. And it was the same with him. Every instinct told her that as she held him close to her, refusing to release him, now or ever.

She had claimed him. And now he was hers.

CHAPTER TWELVE

IN THE PALE dawn light Damiano looked down at the woman on the pillow, overwhelmed with emotion at seeing the face he had expected. The night before had ushered him into a new universe, one that was a mystery to him. In a moment she would awaken and he would see in her eyes the answer to the question that tortured him.

Her eyes opened, and she smiled.

'Hello,' she said.

'Hello.'

'It's like meeting as strangers. You'll never look the same to me again.'

'We're not strangers,' he said at once. 'I knew who you were as soon as I saw your mouth. But what about you? My face was almost completely covered. How could you have recognised me?'

'Because of this,' she said, taking his hand and running her finger over the little scar. 'I knew you as soon as I saw that scar, in the first few minutes.'

'You knew?' His voice was tense. 'You knew it was me all the time?'

'Or I wouldn't have made love to you.'

'I've wanted you too much for too long. Last night you took the decision right out of my hands.'

'Good. You kept me waiting too long. I know we made a deal but things changed, and it was time to renegotiate.'

'What—exactly—changed?' he asked, as though nervous of the answer.

'I found that I wanted you more than I'd ever dreamed would happen. You began to matter to me in—all sorts of ways.'

Still she didn't speak of love, hoping that he would say it first.

'It's the same with me,' he said. 'At first our marriage just seemed something I did for Pietro. I was really marrying you for myself, but I couldn't admit it. It would have meant that I was losing control.'

'Yes, you like to be in command, don't you? Why does that matter so much?'

'I could say that it's the most efficient method of getting what I want,' he said with a touch of wry humour. 'If a man can count on getting his own way, he'd have to be a saint not to. And I'm no saint, as I don't need to tell you.'

'No, you certainly don't need to tell me. But

trying to take command doesn't always make you the victor, and it can turn people against you.'

'I am what I am. I can't change now.'

'But why? I know you've got businesses to run, but I feel it's more than that.'

He was silent for a moment before saying quietly, 'If I told you what makes me this way you might not believe me.'

'Try.'

Again he was silent and she wondered if he meant to answer at all, but at last he uttered one word.

'Fear.'

'Did you say fear?' she asked, wondering if she'd heard him right.

'Yes.'

'You're right, it's hard to believe. People are afraid of you, not you of them.'

'It's not people who scare me, but life. When things seem at their best there's always something nasty waiting just around the corner. A wise man takes control as soon as possible, so that he has a defence.'

'But does he?' she asked gently. 'The disasters waiting around the corner are always the last thing you expected.' She touched his face. 'You're thinking of Gina, aren't you? You were so happy, and then she died.'

She heard him take a long breath. He was gazing at her as though he'd seen an astounding revelation.

'How right I was to want you,' he said. 'There's nothing I couldn't tell you, because you understand everything perfectly.'

'It wasn't hard to work out,' she said. 'I knew that Gina had been your life, and in some ways she still is.'

'But it wasn't just her loss. It was the way it happened, dying in childbirth when things might have been so different. Keeping control seemed the only way to feel safe. But then there was you and suddenly everything was different. With you I could believe again that the world can be a good place.'

She smiled gently. 'Shall we make it a good place again now?'

He took her in his arms. 'I think that's a wonderful idea.'

This lovemaking was as beautiful as the last, but with the difference that now they knew each other better, knew that they were set on a road that would lead them to happiness.

Afterwards he slept, and she lay watching him. His face was totally relaxed and contented, like a man who had found peace and happiness at last.

And that was what he had told her. He hadn't spoken of love, but he'd said she made the world a good place. They had found each other in desire but that alone was not enough. For a true marriage there must be the closeness of the heart.

But now his words implied that love was there, waiting for them.

'I can be patient,' she whispered. 'Our time is coming.'

She leaned down to drop a light kiss on his mouth. He didn't awaken, but a smile transformed his face. Somewhere, deep inside the place where he was now, he knew she had kissed him, and was happy.

Happy, she thought. Have I ever been as happy as I am now? Will I ever be as happy again? Yes. When we admit our love to each other my life will reach its peak.

On their first morning she'd ventured to give him a gentle kiss as he slept, then backed off quickly so that he shouldn't discover her. Now she no longer had to fear, and she could allow herself the luxury of laying her face against his, sending him a silent message with her lips.

At once he began to smile and a soft chuckle broke from him.

'You just don't give up, do you?' he murmured.

'Nope. That's why I always win.'

'You think you won?'

'Well, I didn't lose.'

'Perhaps we both won.'

'Yes,' she murmured. 'Oh, yes.'

The next few minutes were a delight. If she could have stayed there with him all day she would gladly have done so, and her heart and senses told her he felt the same.

'I suppose we've got to get up,' she murmured at last, wrapped in his arms. 'There's so much to do.'

'*We've* got a lot to do,' he said. 'But it'll have to wait until tonight.'

It was time to remove the masks of passionate lovers, and assume those of respectable parents. It was hard but they managed it at breakfast, each taking a polite interest in Mario and Charlie's activities at the hotel, but giving most of their attention to Pietro.

Afterwards they both joined him as he walked the short distance to school.

At the gate they waved him goodbye, then looked at each other. Alone at last.

'There's a café just along there,' Damiano said.

They found the little place in the next alley, ordered coffee and sat sipping it contentedly.

'Why was Pietro giving us those funny looks?' Damiano asked.

'We've never both seen him to school before. I think he's wondering if something is different.'

'Oh, yes, something's different.' His eyes met hers. 'Everything is different.'

She nodded.

'You're a clever, scheming woman,' he said, speaking with a smile that robbed his words of any offence. 'Last night—you set the whole thing up, didn't you?'

'Mmm, I may have anticipated a few things.'

'A few? You conned me into thinking you wouldn't be there, then you turned up pretending to be someone else. Was I not supposed to recognise you?'

'You were bound to recognise me after a few minutes. My mouth, my voice—but you didn't have to admit you knew me. It made us both free of the past and free for the future.' She chuckled. 'I was getting fed up with you being so restrained and virtuous. All those weeks we'd been married and you never—well, I reckoned it was about time I taught you a lesson.'

'You certainly did that,' he said with feeling. 'But did you really blame me for not making love to you?'

'Of course I did. It was insulting.'

'But it was your doing.'

'Me? Did I ask you to keep your distance?'

'In effect yes, when you proclaimed that you didn't love me.'

'I said that to Imelda, to shut her up. Surely you realised that?'

'Yes, and if you'd left it there I might not have worried. But you also said you were perfectly safe

from anything I could do to make you love me.
You sounded so confident. I knew you weren't
marrying me for love—'

'Any more than you were marrying me for
love,' she reminded him. 'It was all for Pietro.'

'Not quite all. Mostly it was for him, but there
was something about you that I wanted, right
from the start. You reached out to him so warmly
that I found myself wondering how it would be if
you reached out to me, then finding that I wanted
you to do that. But you were always so cool and
controlled—'

'Because I thought that was what you wanted.
We agreed how it should be.'

'We said the right words, but things don't always turn out according to the words.'

'I know,' she said. 'You say all sorts of things,
like how certain you are that you'll never care for
someone, but then—'

'But then?' There was a new note in his voice
that might have been hope.

'Then—things happen,' she said carefully.
'People start to look different, and you wonder
if they really are different, or whether they're just
wearing another mask.'

'So you try on a few different masks of your
own, and see how they react,' he said. 'And then?'

'Then you know a little more about them and
about yourself.'

'And what do you do with your new knowledge?' he mused. 'Perhaps you use it to catch your husband at a disadvantage.'

'No, you use it to find out what he wants.'

He regarded her intently. 'And when you know that?'

'It can take time to be sure.'

'Don't play with me, Sally. I gave myself away very completely last night. I knew it was you and nothing could have stopped me from making love to you, especially when I understood that was what you wanted.' His voice became suddenly uneasy. 'It was, wasn't it?'

'Oh, yes, it was,' she assured him.

He reached out to take her hand. 'I'm glad it all happened. I should have known I could rely on you to find the way. I've been so confused. When I started to—' He hesitated.

Started to love me, she thought. Please say it.

'When I started to—have feelings for you I tried to deny them. I felt guilty.'

'Because of Gina.'

'Yes. She gave me everything. It felt like a betrayal to love anyone else. But now—'

'It's not a betrayal,' she said urgently. 'Because you haven't stopped loving her, and I hope you never will.'

'You actually hope—?'

'You still owe her your love and loyalty, and

I'll never try to change that. You have us both, and you always will. Damiano, you have nothing to feel guilty about. Nothing.'

It might have been a risk to speak to him in such a way, but her instincts told her the opposite was true. By confirming his link with Gina she was setting him free to love herself.

'Do you mean that?' he murmured. 'That I'll always have you both?'

'Yes, I mean it. Can't you tell?'

'I can believe it if you say it, and I want to believe it with all my heart.'

'Then believe me. I mean it and I always will. The path ahead is one that the two of us, with Gina and Pietro, will travel together.'

He didn't answer in words, but he took her hand and lowered his head to lay his lips against it.

'Thank you,' he whispered.

'People are staring at you,' she said.

'Let them stare. Let the whole world know how I feel about you.'

But how is that? she thought. Say the word love. Please say it.

'Perhaps we'd better go,' he said.

They walked home by the Grand Canal. Spring was reaching its height and the sun was shining as never before. Watching it glitter on the water, she felt as though the whole world was full of sunshine.

* * *

In the weeks that followed it seemed as though every part of her life was climaxing in triumph. Charlie had settled into his hotel training better than she could have hoped.

'He's doing well,' Mario told her. 'Of course, the fact that two pretty young waitresses are sighing for him has nothing to do with it.'

'At least he's happy.' She laughed.

Summer was coming. The beautiful city glowed. Every day there were new celebrations, often involving dances at the hotels. Not all of them were masked, but they usually involved fancy costumes.

One day there was a glamorous wedding in the hotel chapel, followed by a magnificent ball, to which Damiano and Sally were invited.

She wore the dazzling red and blue dress that she'd worn before, but without the mask that had covered so much of her face. Instead she settled for one that only came down to the end of her nose, and left the lower half of her face free.

'Good thinking,' Damiano told her. 'Otherwise I might forget who you are.'

'Just try it,' she threatened, laughing. 'If you want to get thumped.'

'Being thumped by you might be interesting. I must try it some time.'

They enjoyed a few dances together before

separating to do their duty as hosts. Sally had a friendly chat with the bride before turning away and nearly colliding with a man in an Arlecchino costume and no mask.

'I'm sorry,' he said, steadying her. 'That was clumsy of me.'

'You're English.'

'Yes. And so must you be. I'm so glad to meet you. My Italian is terrible. I never understand a word anybody says. How do you manage in this country?'

'I'm lucky enough to have an Italian husband. He translates for me when I need it.'

'Is he here tonight?'

'Yes, over there. He's taken his mask off, and he's standing by the door.'

Her companion glanced over to where she indicated. Then he tensed.

'That's your husband?'

'Yes.'

'Damiano Ferrone?'

'Yes.' His eyes were beginning to alarm her. More alarming still was the way he began to laugh.

'What is it?' she demanded.

'So you're Pietro's stepmother. Well, well!'

'What do you mean by that?'

'How do you get on with that boy?'

'Very well. He's a lovely child.'

For some reason this seemed to amuse the man even more. Shaking with laughter, he rose and made his way out of the door into the garden. Annoyed, she followed him.

'Is there something funny about me being fond of my stepson? My husband loves him and so do I.'

'Your husband loves him. Oh, yes, that's true. And do you know why?'

'Why? Because Pietro's his son, and because he loved his first wife, and that child is her legacy.'

'No way. He was taken in by the oldest trick in the book. She said the baby was his, but it wasn't. He trusted her. More fool him.'

'What are you saying?' she gasped incredulously.

'I'm saying that kid isn't his.'

'Stop talking nonsense,' she snapped. 'Of course Pietro is his son.'

He thrust his face close to hers and spoke in a rasp.

'Pietro's real father was my brother. He and Gina slept together the night they met, and pretty often after that. Then she found herself pregnant, but he died two days later in a boating accident. And the next thing we heard she was marrying Ferrone. You don't have to be a genius to work out what happened. She had to find a father for that baby so she jumped into Ferrone's bed.'

Sally wanted to scream *No! No! No!* It isn't possible!

But there in her mind was the memory of Damiano, his voice filled with emotion, telling her of the first time Gina had come to him.

'I thought I'd lost her for ever. But on the night of the ball a miracle happened.That night she became mine. She gave herself to me with all the love in her nature.'

But her love had gone to another man, and she had made shameless use of Damiano's adoration. Sally could no longer tell herself that it wasn't true.

'Why did you come here tonight?' she demanded.

'Because the time has come to tell him. I was about to make a deal with a very wealthy man, until Ferrone stepped in and made him a better offer. I've taken quite a loss, and I'm going to make him sorry.'

'No, I won't let you.'

'You couldn't stop me. Look.'

He took out a photograph and thrust it into her hand. Looking at it, Sally felt all her nightmares come true.

There in the picture was Gina, her arms around

a young man who was also embracing her. But it was the man's face that devastated her.

It was Pietro's face. Even given the difference in ages the likeness was so great that she could no longer doubt this was the boy's father. Her last hope died.

'With that picture I have all the proof I need,' he said. 'I'm looking forward to showing it to him.'

Her answer was to tear the picture into little scraps.

'Now where's your proof?' she snapped.

'You don't think I was stupid enough to bring only one? I've got another. And it's too late for you to stop me. Look behind you.'

She did so and saw something that horrified her.

Damiano was standing there, and from his stony look she could tell that he'd heard every word.

'Show me the other picture,' he said in a voice of ice.

With a cynical expression the man drew out the copy and thrust it at Damiano.

Watching Damiano's face as he studied the picture, Sally wished she could fade away to nothing. He had no choice but to admit the truth.

'Look at my brother,' the man sneered. 'He's

got the same face you see on that boy. Now what
are you going to do?'

'Nothing,' Damiano said. 'If you were hoping to give me a shock you're going to be disap-
pointed. This is no surprise to me. Now get out.'

'You think you've won, don't you?' the man
sneered. 'But the truth is still the truth and it'll
always be there.' He raised his voice. 'You're not
that boy's father. You never were and you never
will be. And you'll always have to live with it.'

'Get out of here,' Damiano said in a voice of
ominous quiet, 'before I make you sorry you were
born.'

The man fled. Damiano went to sit on the stone
bench, dropping his head into his hands. Sally
went to sit beside him and put her arms around
him.

'I'm sorry,' she whispered. 'I'm so sorry. I wish
there was something I could do to take this pain
away from you. You said it came as no surprise
to you, but I can't believe you actually knew.'

He raised his head to look at her.

'No, I didn't know, but I'd suspected. Gina became pregnant so quickly after her return that I
was bound to wonder.'

'All these years—'

'I refused to believe it because I didn't want to.
And it seemed cruel to suspect her when she was

dead and couldn't defend herself. Now I know and everything is different.'

Was there no way to ease his pain? she wondered. But then something came back to her. Incredibly, she knew something that might help him. After a moment's hesitation she came to a sudden fierce decision.

'Yes, everything is different,' she said. 'In one way—' she paused, taking a deep breath to summon up her courage '—in one way, things are better.'

He stared.

'Better? What can you mean?'

'You told me once that you felt to blame for her death, that you gave her the child whose birth killed her. But you didn't.'

'I—'

'It wasn't your fault, Damiano, you must understand that. You said the feeling of guilt haunted you, but you have nothing to feel guilty about. You didn't kill her. *It wasn't your fault.*'

Still he stared, thunderstruck.

'It'll take time for you to get your head around it,' she said, 'but you'll find that the darkness soon starts to lift.'

He took her face between his hands.

'You say the darkness will lift, but I know now that that began to happen the day you came into my life. I discovered something else tonight, listening to you. You fought that man, to let me keep my dreams of Gina, although she must have always been a trouble to you.'

'I'd have done anything to stop that man hurting you.'

'Even if it meant you paid a price?'

'Even then. Because I love you with all my heart. I hoped you'd come to understand that without my saying it.'

'I've been so blind. I never realised—to think the truth about you—about us—has always been there, facing me. To have your love—' He was suddenly tense. 'I do have it, don't I? You did say that?'

'You have my love now and you always will have.'

'And you will always have mine. It's as though my heart and mind have suddenly become clear, seeing and understanding everything about you, and me—and Gina. This must have been what she wanted to tell me on her death bed. I vowed to protect our son, but she was going to tell me he wasn't mine.'

'No,' Sally said quickly. 'She would never have been so cruel. She was going to tell you that she loved you. You saved her from disaster and made her last months happier than she could have dreamed. In the last moments of her life her heart was yours.'

He stared. 'You can't be sure of that.'

'I can because I can't imagine knowing you and not loving you. She loved you, my darling. And she wanted you to know that, so that if this day ever arrived you would still have her love to rely on.'

'But now I have yours. You might have seized the chance to kick her out of my life and own me completely. Instead—'

'I don't want to own you. I want you to give me your love freely, or not at all.'

'Has there ever been another woman as generous as you?' he breathed.

'It happens when a woman truly loves a man.'

But Damiano didn't believe her. In his eyes and his newly awakened heart the generosity she showered on him was hers alone, and he would cling to her for his survival. There could be no life without her. But with her a glorious future was opening before him.

'What about Pietro?' she asked. 'Will this affect your love for him?'

'No, because I've always had this slight suspicion that he wasn't mine. I couldn't be sure but I came to feel a bond between us that didn't depend on my being his father in every sense. That bond has grown over the years, and it won't die now.'

'Will you tell him?'

'One day I may have to. If that man comes

back I don't want Pietro taken by surprise. But not yet. Let's go and say goodnight to him.'

But as they passed Pietro's room they stopped, appalled by the sound of violent sobbing coming from inside. Damiano threw open the door and they saw the child lying on the bed, his face buried in the pillow.

'Pietro,' his father cried, dropping down beside him and trying to take him in his arms.

'Go away,' Pietro cried. 'You're not my father.'

'Of course I am. Come here.'

But Pietro fought him off.

'You're not!' he screamed. 'I was outside, I heard what they said. You're not my father, you don't love me. You don't, you don't, *you don't*.'

Damiano looked up at Sally, his face full of desperation. She took a deep breath. Their whole future depended on this moment. Sitting down on Pietro's other side, she took him in her arms. He made no attempt to fight her as he'd fought Damiano.

'You're wrong, my darling. Papa does love you, and that's what makes him your father. The rest—whether he fathered you at birth—simply doesn't matter. After all, I didn't give birth to you, but you call me Mamma because you know I love you as a mother, and you've accepted me as your mother, which means all the world to me.

'Your father here has loved you all your life,

because you're a wonderful son. That's what makes him your father—your father of the heart.'

Pietro looked up at her, clearly taking in what she was saying, and mulling it over seriously.

'What happens now is up to you,' she told him. 'Do you accept him as your father, or will you refuse and break his heart?'

Pietro looked back and forth between them. Damiano was watching Sally as though she held all his life in her hands.

Which in a way she did, she thought. She gave him a significant glance, nodding in Pietro's direction, hoping he would understand.

He did. He took the child's hand and said gently, 'Will you accept me as your father, if I beg you to?'

Slowly Pietro nodded. The next moment he was enfolded in Damiano's arms.

'Thank you,' she told the child. 'That means everything to Papa, because he loves you more than anyone in the world, and he always will.'

'But not more than you,' Pietro said innocently from within the shelter of Damiano's embrace.

'Much more than me.' She met Damiano's eyes and mouthed, 'Tell him.'

He tensed, sensing how much this mattered but unwilling to say the words. He knew now that he could never love anyone more than her, even if he'd only just realised how deeply.

'Say it,' she urged silently again.

'It's true,' he told Pietro. 'You come first with me, and—and you always will.'

Sally was smiling with approval and the sensation made him dizzy with relief and happiness. He was a man who'd always insisted on being in control, but now even that side of him was glad to yield to her. He was in her power, and for the first time in his life he didn't mind the subjugation.

She was stronger than he was. She would keep him safe. He was content.

The three of them remained together for an hour. It was only when Pietro had gone to sleep that they could say things that needed to be said.

'Do you like the mask I'm wearing now?' she whispered.

But he shook his head.

'To me you have never worn a mask,' he said. 'I looked at you and saw the woman I was fated to love for the rest of my life. That is no mask, and it never will be.'

He drew her closer into his arms.

'*Te vojo ben,*' he said, uttering the Venetian words of love that she had longed to hear. '*Te vojo ben.*'

* * * * *

COMING NEXT MONTH FROM

HARLEQUIN®

Romance

Available September 2, 2014

#4439 INTERVIEW WITH A TYCOON
Cara Colter

Journalist Stacy needs a big story—so she tracks down eligible bachelor and infamous recluse Kiernan. But soon, Stacy concerns herself with healing the heart of this controlled, commanding man....

#4440 HER BOSS BY ARRANGEMENT
Teresa Carpenter

Studio director Garret can't afford distractions—especially when they're as tempting as gorgeous event coordinator Tori. Tori knows men like Garret are bad news...but her heart has other ideas.

#4441 IN HER RIVAL'S ARMS
Alison Roberts

He may bring bad news, but when Dominic walks into Suzanna's shop she can't control her heart. Could ending up in her rival's arms be the best decision she's ever made?

#4442 FROZEN HEART, MELTING KISS
Ellie Darkins

Maya has one great passion—cooking! Her new client Will may be hard to please, but working together is shaping up to be more delicious than they ever imagined....

YOU CAN FIND MORE INFORMATION
ON UPCOMING HARLEQUIN® TITLES,
FREE EXCERPTS AND MORE AT
WWW.HARLEQUIN.COM.

HRLPCNM0814

LARGER-PRINT BOOKS!

GET 2 FREE LARGER-PRINT NOVELS PLUS
2 FREE GIFTS!

HARLEQUIN®

Romance

From the Heart, For the Heart

YES! Please send me 2 FREE LARGER-PRINT Harlequin® Romance novels and my 2 FREE gifts (gifts are worth about $10). After receiving them, if I don't wish to receive any more books, I can return the shipping statement marked "cancel." If I don't cancel, I will receive 4 brand-new novels every month and be billed just $4.84 per book in the U.S. or $5.24 per book in Canada. That's a savings of at least 19% off the cover price! It's quite a bargain! Shipping and handling is just 50¢ per book in the U.S. and 75¢ per book in Canada.* I understand that accepting the 2 free books and gifts places me under no obligation to buy anything. I can always return a shipment and cancel at any time. Even if I never buy another book, the two free books and gifts are mine to keep forever.

119/319 HDN F43Y

Name _____ (PLEASE PRINT) _____

Address _____ Apt. #

City _____ State/Prov. _____ Zip/Postal Code

Signature (if under 18, a parent or guardian must sign)

Mail to the **Harlequin® Reader Service:**
IN U.S.A.: P.O. Box 1867, Buffalo, NY 14240-1867
IN CANADA: P.O. Box 609, Fort Erie, Ontario L2A 5X3

Want to try two free books from another line?
Call 1-800-873-8635 or visit www.ReaderService.com.

* Terms and prices subject to change without notice. Prices do not include applicable taxes. Sales tax applicable in N.Y. Canadian residents will be charged applicable taxes. Offer not valid in Quebec. This offer is limited to one order per household. Not valid for current subscribers to Harlequin Romance Larger-Print books. All orders subject to credit approval. Credit or debit balances in a customer's account(s) may be offset by any other outstanding balance owed by or to the customer. Please allow 4 to 6 weeks for delivery. Offer available while quantities last.

HRLP13R

Read on for an exclusive sneak preview of
INTERVIEW WITH A TYCOON by Cara Colter…

KIERNAN WAITED FOR it to happen. All his strength had not been enough to hold the lid on the place that contained the grief within him.

The touch of her hand, the look in her eyes, and his strength had abandoned him, and he had told her all of it: his failure and his powerlessness.

Now, sitting beside her, her hand in his, the wetness of her hair resting on his shoulder, he waited for everything to fade: the white-topped mountains that surrounded him, the feel of the hot water against his skin, the way her hand felt in his.

He waited for all that to fade, and for the darkness to take its place, to ooze through him like thick black sludge freed from a containment pond, blotting out all else.

Instead, astounded, Kiernan became *more* aware of everything around him, as if he were soaking up life through his pores, breathing in glory through his nose, becoming drenched in light instead of darkness.

He started to laugh.

"What?" she asked, a smile playing across the lovely fullness of her lips.

"I just feel alive. For the last few days, I have felt alive. And I don't know if that's a good thing or a bad thing."

His awareness shifted to her, and being with her seemed to fill him to overflowing.

He dropped his head over hers and took her lips. He kissed her with warmth and with welcome, a man who had thought he was dead discovering not just that he lived but, astonishingly, that he wanted to live.

Stacy returned his kiss, her lips parting under his, her hands twining around his neck, pulling him in even closer to her.

There was gentle welcome. She had seen all of him, he had bared his weakness and his darkness to her, and still he felt only acceptance from her.

But acceptance was slowly giving way to something else. There was hunger in her, and he sensed an almost savage need in her to go to the place a kiss like this took a man and a woman.

With great reluctance he broke the kiss, cupped her cheeks in his hands and looked down at her.

He felt as if he was memorizing each of her features: the green of those amazing eyes, her dark brown hair curling even more wildly from the steam of the hot spring, the swollen plumpness of her lips, the whiteness of her skin.

"It's too soon for this," he said, his voice hoarse.

"I know," she said, and her voice was raw, too.

Don't miss this heart-wrenching story, available September 2014 from Harlequin® Romance.